Praise for Ace Baker's Writ

"The Killing Jar"

"A wonderful story of love, heartbreak, and redemption, all sliding past each other in overlapping layers of depth and meaning." —Diana Gabaldon, author of the *Outlander* series

"This story is a tour de force that left me breathless and awed by the indelible images it thrust into my awareness. It's a searing piece of writing--terse, taut, and terrific in its brilliant intensity, with the poetic commentaries falling like sparks from a brilliant rocket. A stand-out winner by anyone's standards." —Jack Whyte, author of *The Camulod Chronicles*

"Plow Breaks Soil"

"Big Red Schoolhouse (the poem included in "Plow Breaks Soil") keeps us up to our elbows in the muck of the moment...the poem is dynamic and dramatic in its details, as elegiac as it is realistic and beautifully sequenced though stanza and line...a choreographed chaos of feelings and action, dominated by a double dimension of obligation..." —George McWhirter, Vancouver's first Poet Laureate

"Graphic and painful, but so wonderful to read. Really interesting and compelling story." —Geraldine MacDonald, *Blank Spaces* fiction contest judge

"Menos Coca, Más Cacao"

"Now that I know that Ace is also a poet, it makes sense because I noticed the rhythm and the flow and the pacing." —Rachel Laverdiere, editor *Barren Magazine*

HOW TO MAKE A KILLING JAR

Stories

ACE BAKER

Kathy,
Thanks so much for the endless hours of effort and support for writers! It's a real joy for me to be able to give back as a presenter this year, thanks to you and your committee!
Wings to Victory,
Ace

CHICKEN HOUSE PRESS

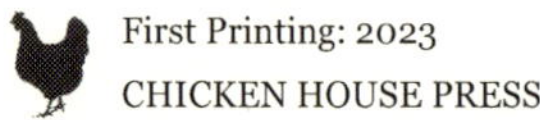

First Printing: 2023
CHICKEN HOUSE PRESS

ISBN trade paperback edition: 978-1-990336-54-6

Library and Archives Canada Cataloguing in Publication
CIP data on file with the National Library and Archives

"Choose Something Like a Star" *The Complete Poems of Robert Frost*, Henry Holt & Co, New York City (1949)

Chicken House Press
282906 Normanby/Bentinck Townline
Durham, Ontario, Canada, N0G 1R0

www.chickenhousepress.ca

This book of short stories is for my loving wife, Anna. You have been my unwavering support and inspiration, my biggest fan, and my greatest love. I dedicate this book to you with all my heart.

CONTENTS

HOW TO MAKE A KILLING JAR

Ace Baker

“We delight in the beauty of the butterfly, but rarely admit the changes it has gone through to achieve that beauty.” Maya Angelou

MY SINGAPORE GARDEN

It sounds like the beginning of a terrible joke: *What's black and white and green all over?*

For me, back then, the answer was a paradox: boldness and brokenness; an open door and a closed cage; a paradise and a prison.

In Singapore, black and whites are buildings linked to a colonial past. The British built them, mostly to house high-ranking military officers in the early to mid-1900s. Their name connects to the contrast between dark wood beams and whitewashed walls. Years after the end of World War II, many were renovated and rented out for homes, for businesses, for restaurants.

Others, like the one we're staring at right now, have been empty for years. And in a hot, humid country where any seed that drops to the ground will grow, what happens after years of neglect is inevitable.

Nature takes back what's hers.

This black and white has a tree growing in the centre of the building, branches stretching skyward, punching through orange ceramic roof tiles. That orange roof makes way for red leaves. The tree is called Flame of the Forest, and, in full bloom, it's an inferno in the sky.

The building is being destroyed by fire but is still standing.

It's a paradox, *non*?

And the roof is all we can see from the road in Rochester Park. There's a fifteen-foot fence surrounding the condemned building, which lies there peacefully, a sleeping ancestor. It will remain undisturbed until a higher purpose is dreamed up for it by a modern government.

Or a pair of 16-year-old girls.

This century-old building is well-built and strong. It's still standing even as nature spreads through open doors, open windows, and now, an open roof. But the new fence has been more hastily constructed. Thin, interlocking aluminum panels are dotted with rusting rivets, and it takes only a few experimental presses of our palms to find a loose panel, one that can be pushed in to allow a few skinny bodies to slip through.

And that's how a French Canadian and an Indo Singaporean found themselves inside a British property.

And we hit it off right away. She taught me Singlish; I taught her Québecois. She explained the differences between lah and leh and lor, and I explained the difference between "mun tree all" (the English pronunciation) and "mow ray al," the actual pronunciation of where I'm from —Montréal.

We'd go over crucial phrases, like how to say good-looking guy or good-looking girl—*yandou* and *chibou* for her, *le chum* and *la blonde* for me. And we learned how the Singlish phrase for being horny—*hamsap* ("salty wet") sounded mostly like a female reference and the Québecois phrase—having "*la mine dans le crayon*" (lead in your pencil) sounded mostly male.

An educational experience, to be sure.

Rewind.

I know you're wondering how the two of us got together. The quick answer? Our fathers.

My dad is an ICT geek, and his boss told him one day he was needed overseas for a collaborative project at Fusionopolis—a state-of-the-art research facility in Singapore.

After a video call to his Singaporean contact, and after learning that he *also* had a 16-year-old daughter, and me being on summer vacation and all—well, let's just say it wasn't difficult convincing me to accompany him to an island paradise.

Baljit, Bal, his new co-worker's daughter, wouldn't be on vacation anytime soon, but there would still be plenty of time for her to play tour guide to me after school and on weekends.

Fast forward.

We're inside and the property is thick with foliage—

overgrown grasses and weeds, and plants of all kinds. To my untrained eye, it's hard to tell what's what.

But Bal tromps a path for us until we're dead centre, staring up at sunlight peeking through the gaps in the ceiling and roof. A tree piercing through from below, sunlight piercing through from above—and I got the distinct impression that this was a battle that Mother Nature would eventually win.

That first day, we trampled it all—every bit of green growing inside that building—all except that Flame of the Forest, of course.

And it took forever, and we came back all sweaty and thirsty and full of dreams of rebuilding that home around that magnificent tree, respecting nature while living with it.

Can you imagine? A centre courtyard with that tree in the middle, leaves lighting up the space, and the building constructed in a rectangle around it.

Most days, we skipped the tourist traps and returned to that black and white—cleaning it up, clearing it out, making sure not to make too much noise so as to gain attention from anyone passing by.

Making it our home.

Bit by bit, we brought in tools. Ones we purchased, like the fold-up shovel or the rake with a telescopic handle. Ones we didn't, like the straw broom discarded by a worker on the side of the road or the pots discarded by locals, the big ones, that we tipped over and used as makeshift stools.

Before long, we'd hung up hammocks, whacked back

weeds to the fence edges, and cleared a spot where we could grow our own garden. I decided I could put in some extra time while Bal was in school, and she could join me when she finished her classes.

And that was my first mistake.

My second was not taking a good look around before slipping through the fence.

We'd hacked away the tall weeds and grasses, so I decided to start clearing our garden space of everything else. We wanted a clean slate for what would become our masterpiece. I pulled over a pot to sit on and bent over, my right hand loosening soil with a hand spade, my left tugging tiny weeds out, being sure to get the roots with them.

I hadn't gotten far before I felt myself pushed hard to the ground from behind. The stranger was on top of me immediately, pressing the trunk of his body against mine, pinning me to the earth. His branch of an elbow pinned my right arm to the ground while tendril fingers stretched over my lips to keep me from screaming. His other hand pinned my left arm, and he lay on top of me, pressing, pressing, until I struggled no more.

Then he raised himself up, reaching to tug his shorts down—and I heard a sickening *SMACK!*

His body flattened out on top of mine again and lay there unmoving.

I stared over his shoulder, directly into the eyes of Bal, holding our shovel in her hands like a baseball bat.

"Get him off me," I yelled.

And she did, and rolled him over, and gasped aloud at

the sight that greeted her. The bone, caved in, an emptiness. The flesh, carved open, an ugliness. And out of that hollow, blood coursing over a jagged rock that lay close by.

No breathing.

No pulse.

The pool of blood expanding.

Some Caucasian hippie bum—long blonde hair in dreadlocks; sun, moon, and stars shorts; and a tie-dye shirt. Head now covered in blood.

And we did not speak.

Bal just jammed that shovel into the ground and began digging a trench the length of his body. When she got tired, I took over, and when I got tired, she finished the job. She searched his pockets and backpack and relieved him of his wallet and passport before the two of us pushed and rolled that body into the pit. She dumped his backpack at his feet and then she nodded at the shovel, and I began piling dirt on the corpse. I stopped almost immediately, went over and grabbed a packet of the darkest seeds of ours that I could find, and scattered them over his pale arms, hands, feet, and head.

Black on white. Black and white.

"The seeds will grow and feed on the body," I said. "Maybe that way, some small good thing will come of this." And I spread more over his clothes, emptying the package.

"I felt guilty leaving you to do the work all by yourself, so I decided to ditch school," Bal said.

"Lucky for me."

And I sat there, my shorts covered in mud, my blouse covered in blood.

Mud and blood—and no plausible excuse to explain it away.

"Are you all right staying here while I run to Star Vista?"

I nodded.

And before Bal slipped through the fence again, she told me to sit right against the loose panel and not move until I heard her voice again.

And I did.

With my back pressed to the fence, I sat staring at the dirt mound, picturing what would happen. The seeds would grow. The seeds would suck sustenance from a dead body. From blood in that body. Would it affect their colour? Would there be wildfire flowers below to match the Flame of the Forest leaves above?

And I watched that mound of dirt. Would it move? Did we really kill him, or would he suddenly gasp awake, suck dirt into his lungs, and send arms popping out of the earth like some B-grade zombie movie?

And me, the only one here.

And I hugged myself tightly, my thoughts alternating between visions of my own beautiful Singapore flower garden and that horror movie starring Bal and me, that hungry hippie zombie hoping to feast on our brains as payback for spilling his.

Before long, she returned, shopping bag in hand. First, she pulled out a large package of wet wipes and cleaned blood spatter from my hair, my face, my neck. Then clay from my legs and ankles.

"Stand up and strip," she ordered.

And I did. My blouse and shorts formed a pool at my feet. She handed me the t-shirt first and then the shorts that she'd just purchased at the mall, and I quickly slipped into them. Then she piled the bloody, muddy clothing and wet wipes into the shopping bag and tied it tightly.

"You keep his money," she said, handing it to me. "I'll take care of the rest." Then she took the wad of bills back quickly and peeled off a few, handing the rest to me again. "That should cover the clothing."

It wasn't far to walk back to the grounds of her building complex. When we got there, five smoking metal drums greeted us. A scattering of people burned things in the barrels.

"Superstition," Bal said. "They're burning fake paper money, fake paper cars—things for the afterlife for the hungry ghosts of ancestors." And she walked up to one and tossed the ID and passport into the fire below. Together, we stood over them, watching as flames slowly curled the pages of the passport, slowly melted the plastic of the ID, eventually making it into some unrecognizable mess.

Just like his body would be, eventually, I thought.

And we took the elevator to her place on the twenty-fourth floor. And as soon as we got inside, Bal walked straight to the garbage chute and sent the plastic bag of clothes hurtling down.

"Garbage from lunch," she said, when her mom looked over.

And I marvelled at how calm she was, how smoothly

she dished out the lies to hide the truth.

Like soil spread over a body.

And at dinner time, she feasted on all the dishes her mother had prepared.

And I didn't.

Days passed, and her calm façade began to fade and crack. I could see the guilt spread through her like bacteria, like some unstoppable disease. She wasn't sleeping. Her studies were suffering. Her parents were likely going to blame me for her poor performance—something like that—and they wouldn't be wrong.

That night, I had a nightmare of my own. I arrived safely back in Canada. I went on with my life as usual. And years later, when I had a husband and family of my own, I got the notification from Singapore police.

Murder.

That jerked me awake.

Bal cracking and spilling the whole story, implicating the both of us. And—they have the death penalty in Singapore, don't they?

Daily, I saw her deteriorate, and I became her twin. No sleep, no appetite, no life. And we'd check that fence panel from time to time and make sure that mound of dirt remained undisturbed... except for the seeds beginning to sprout.

As my days in Singapore dwindled and my plane ride

back to Canada approached, she surprised me one night when she whispered to me, "Should we—you know—say something to someone about it? Show them it was self-defence?"

And I knew then my days were numbered. Not just my days in Singapore. My days on Earth.

It's why I decided to steal one of her giant silver hoop earrings.

Her body was darker than caramel but lighter than a midnight black, and I loved how the silver shone against her ebony skin. I suspected she loved those earrings for much the same reason. So, when one went missing, she noticed.

"Have you seen it?" she asked. "Anywhere?"

And that moment was the one I'd been waiting for, the one I'd been practicing my reaction for. "You're missing it, and you're sure it's nowhere to be found in the house?" Confused look. Eyebrows. Eyebrows.

Then eyes wide. Shocked look. "Bal! What if? I mean, if you dropped it when we went to check on the body at the black and white? It's the only thing that can link you to the crime. We need to get it back."

She nodded. "Tonight," she said. "We'll do it tonight."

And we waited until we heard the snoring from the fathers and not a peep from her mother. It was past midnight, and we quietly slipped out the door, even more carefully than we would slide through the fence panels. There was no one in the elevator, and we breathed a sigh of relief.

We each had flashlights, but we didn't turn them on

until we got inside the fence.

Bal spotted the earring almost immediately, right where I'd placed it. She bent down to pick it up, and I bent down to pick up that sharp stone, *that* sharp stone, the one we'd scrubbed clean and left as a reminder to be careful.

And as she rose, I hammered it down, over and over again, feeling her ceramic skull crack and open, brains exposed to the sky, the moonlight shining in.

And I looked at the new trench beside her, the one I'd dug the previous day, and I thought, *What did she think would happen if she acted the way she did?* She left me no choice. Cause and effect. Simple cause and effect.

I did my best not to look at her and felt through her pockets at the same time for her house keys.

Then I rolled her into the trench and I spread the lightest, palest seeds we had over her body. White on black. Black and white. And this time, I tossed the rock in with her. I knew I wouldn't be back.

And after shovelling soil over her, I was sticky and sweaty, blood splashed on my blouse.

But I was prepared this time. I fished out the wet wipes and clothing from my backpack, and cleaned every inch of myself, taking no chances.

Back at her home on the twenty-fourth floor, I unlocked and locked the doors behind me, then slipped the keys into the plastic bag that held my bloody clothing, and sent it all down the garbage chute.

It was just a matter of sneaking into our bedroom, and her side of the bed was already disturbed from her getting up in the middle of the night, so there was nothing left for me to do but wait.

The next morning, I intentionally "slept in." Truth is, I hadn't been able to sleep a wink. But when they woke me and asked where Bal was, I returned to what I've practiced. Confused look. Eyebrow raise. Eyebrow raise.

Eyes wide open. Look over to the right at the empty space in bed. Shift eyes left to right, right to left. Look slightly guilty, but not too guilty.

"What is it? What do you know?" her father shouted.

"I—she—she told me she met this boy. She was sneaking out to meet him. You mean—she's not back?"

And panic ensued. And the police were notified, as I knew they would be. And our flight back home was delayed as they investigated, as I knew it would be.

And they found no leads, as I knew they would not.

And no one will ever ask me that riddle, I know, but I have an answer prepared and rehearsed just in case.

What's black and white and green all over?

1. A black and white. *That* black and white.
2. Those bodies blooming flowers.
3. A seasick zebra.

And there are three possible answers, but really, there's only one.

And years have passed. And each year, in my imagination, I add to the vision of my Singapore garden—new colours, new flowers, spreading and filling that entire space, bright red leaves above and a rainbow below.

Purple morning glories and yellow creeping daisies, orange ixoran and blue spiderworts, lavender touch-me-nots and deep red lipstick plants.

Red.

Like Flame of the Forest.

Like blood.

And I know I'll never see it in person again—everyone knows the biggest mistake you can make is to return to the scene of a crime.

But I'm placing a copy of this story with my will—and it will be read when I pass away.

And at that moment, they'll know who the murderers are, who the murderer is, without a doubt. And they'll find every bit of evidence they need to prosecute.

And they will not be able to prosecute.

It's a paradox, *non*?

COOKIE MONSTER

My daughter, you're a cross-bearer. You know what I mean. You always have something or other you're fighting for, or fighting against. "He sends a cross," you love to say, "but He also sends the strength to bear it."

I don't believe that anymore.

I mean, life has a way of loading that cross onto your back or even nailing you to it, but it's a slow wear, you know, like water on rock, and the rock looks tough and strong and all, but eventually, the water wins out, doesn't it?

It's like dealing with *those* kinds of people—and they can be your friends, your family, your neighbours, even *you* when you're good and fit to be tied and can't stand being in the room with yourself—those kinds of crosses—but my daughter, Felicity, Fe, you just get under the weight of it all and you take it on your shoulders and tread forward, one foot after the other, like breath, like breathing.

And I should know, since I'm one of the weights pushing down on you—we're often at cross currents over some thing or other, but the love still squeezes out from under, eventually. We both get that.

And you can still find time to bake—don't that beat all? I mean, I can just imagine you *that* day, standing next to the stove as the oven timer buzzes...

You take a peek at the wall calendar—the one with the golden retriever puppies on it, well, that, and the date February 14th circled, the day of your fifteenth wedding anniversary—and I can just see the care you'd take with those cookies. You'd slip on your favourite oven mitts, the ones with the faded pink roses, then slide out two trays of chocolate chip cookies, Claude's favourite. Then you'd put in two more of oatmeal raisin. Those would be for Chantelle. I mean, those kids can empty cookie jars in record time—if the dough even makes it to the oven in the first place.

But I'm getting ahead of myself. Back to the crosses you bear. I mean, I don't really know how you do it all—PTA president, charity work, Sunday school, a house and a husband, two kids and a dog—it's a juggling act even Cirque du Soleil might hesitate to take on. The amazing HERdini, the miracle mom—just like Jesus, kind of.

Hey, speaking of which, I got a good one for you—

heard it on the Comedy Channel the other day and thought you'd flip a lid if you'd been there to hear it yourself. I mean, it was a one-liner, but it was good. The guy looked straight at the camera, I mean he looked the camera right in the lens, and said, "Jesus was a cross dresser."

And it kind of rolled over the crowd like a slow wave, gaining speed as it came to shore, then—*splash!*—a kind of eruption in the crowd, like when water smacks against stone. And the thing was, he *knew* what to do. He kind of held off and gave it time to happen. You know, sometimes you just have to give these things time to work.

I think Jesus would kind of like that one too—because it's harmless, but it still gets the point across, you know? I mean, I don't think Jesus would like looking at all these fancy crosses hanging from the necks of Christians nowadays—the constant reminder and all. It'd be like wearing a diamond-studded, solid gold pendant of an airplane or two with 9/11 engraved on it, and then parading around the streets of New York City. Just all in bad taste overall, don't you think?

And speaking of taste, I just can't get those cookies of yours out of my head. How you ever learned to bake like that is beyond me. It certainly wasn't anything I did. But you, you're different.

I can almost see you struggling with that sticky timer, setting it for that second batch and then striding down the hallway, past all those framed family faces watching over you.

You'd whisk into your bedroom and then step right

inside that walk-in closet that's big enough to house a family of four all by itself. Your little frame would rise up on tiptoes, taking down your favourite little black party dress, the one with the bow in front that ever so tastefully blocks out a bit of your cleavage. You'd lay it out neatly on the bed, smoothing out those fine lines of French design. You always did have good taste, in cookies and in fashion.

And to me, it must've been just about that time that the thought crossed your mind.

You reach for the photo album on the nightstand.

Summer in Cancun. Tequila Sunrises with Mike while the two of you watched the kids learn how to fish like locals. A hook with two barbs sticking out on either side, some fishing line, and a Coke can for a reel. Then they just crossed their fingers and prayed a quick prayer—for something, for anything, for a nibble even. But no slippery creatures took the bait that day. You'd never know it from the smiles on their faces.

Winter in Whistler. Snowboarding lessons. Sore bums, clothes soaked clear through, cold to the bones—and loving every minute of it.

Another winter in Hawaii. You and Mike, before kids. Sunrise atop Haleakala—who knew a volcano could be so chilly, right? You told me both of you were shaking blue clear down to your boots, but the teeth stopped chattering as light lit up those other peaks, rimming them with fire.

Oven timer.

And I can see you skipping down the hall to the kitchen. The chocolate chip cookies would be cool by now, so you'd place them in the Elmo cookie jar for Claude. He'd be right tickled.

Then you'd fill the cooling racks with the oatmeal raisin ones fresh out of the oven, and you'd pop in the sugar cookies—Mike and his sweet tooth!—and step back and admire your little assembly line success.

Doorbell.

And it'd be some Jehovah's Witness and you'd actually listen to them and all—not just shut the door in their faces like most do—and you'd just explain that you have your own beliefs and you respect the fact that they have theirs as well, and that would be that, and

And that reminds me—do you know what you get when you cross a Jehovah's Witness and an atheist? Someone who knocks on your door for no apparent reason! I thought you'd like that one.

Anyhow, I see you lock the door behind that JW—I mean the one who had you right in her crosshairs and is now going away empty-handed, empty-souled, but full of joy anyway somehow—and then I see you take the two empty trays and a pair of scissors from the kitchen counter and head back to the bedroom.

And to me, that's when things get weird. I mean, a place for everything and everything in its place, and everyone knows that a bedroom is no place for cookie sheets and scissors.

All the same, I see you place those trays on the bed between the black dress and the photo album. You're sitting up on bed, cross-legged, and taking out four of your favourite photos—you and Mike on a Maui beach, hand in hand; Claude, your eldest, on the day he was born; Chantelle, knees and elbows all scraped up and bleeding on the day the adults were all too busy, so she decided to teach herself to ride that bike, and did; and the one of the four of you together—along with Mickey and Minnie, you know, adults who hide behind false faces. But the kids were glowing like diamonds on velvet.

And then you'd stand again, give that dress a cross look, and smooth out invisible creases some more, letting your fingers suck in the softness of the cloth.

All at once I see you snatch up the scissors and bring them down on that dress, hacking out a large rectangle. You gently place the scrap on the bed, smoothing it out again, laying the photo of you and Mike on the centre of it. Then you'd mutter something poetic or other, maybe like something Ophelia might say in Hamlet: "There's a black picture frame; pray love, remember."

And you'd snip out another shape, this one with a short straight stem and a circular top. Placing Claude's photo in it, you'd say, "A dark sleeping bulb, love; that's for thoughts."

Next, another cutout, a long vertical stem and a short horizontal one, cut from the back of the dress. You'd wrap that one around skinned knees and elbows: "A dark reminder that He isn't always looking out for us. The world sometimes wounds."

And it's true, and I knew you were hurting and I did nothing about it. Nothing at all. I remember you telling me as you were growing up that all girls needed a kryptonite cross to keep Dracula and Superman away. One wanted to suck the life out of you and the other was forever trying to save you from something or other. Cross those up and you'd get some kind of Dracman—a guy who'd be so busy trying to save himself that he'd have no time to muck with the lives of others.

I'm all out of kryptonite crosses.

But I do have another joke for you, and I hope you don't mind. What do you get when you cross an insomniac, a dyslexic, and an agnostic? . . . Someone who stays up all night wondering if there is a DOG!

I mean, Clara told me that one and I almost split a gut —I mean, it was a real knee-slapper—that's what I mean. No offence.

Because it's hard for me to think about what comes next.

Another slash of the scissors, another piece of cloth. This one curved on one end. "A black tongue, for false flattery. Words freely given, but not felt with the heart. I'd have cut out a black heart too, but the world is already filled with them."

Then I see you pull out three pieces of paper and arrange them on that other cookie sheet—the big paper in the middle, the two smaller ones at either end.

Oven timer.

You're moving much more slowly now, one tray in each hand, making sure not to spill the contents or have the papers fly up as you make your way down the hall and into the kitchen.

Gently, you'd place the trays on top of the stove. Then you'd transfer the raisin oatmeal cookies to the Big Bird cookie jar, and set the sugar cookies on the cooling rack. You'd slip in the tray of photos first, and take a final glance at the other cookie sheet.

The newspaper clipping in the centre has a photo of a smiling Mike and kids, but a headline that reads, "Sea to Sky Highway Claims Three More Lives." The two notes—one at either end—are, one, a letter from your husband's lover that you found while going through his things last Tuesday, and two, a card you'd received from your lover that very day.

I can feel you close the oven door, keep any kind of warmth away from you. I see you watch through the window as the edges curl and darken before the blackness creeps inside.

There's an urgency now, as you race down the hallway back to the bedroom. You're caught in the crossfire of family, you, others, and caught in the cross fire of the church too.

When they find you, you're wearing that little black dress, the holey one that's been slashed to bits. An outline of soft pink flesh in the shape of a cross glows up at the investigators. Two trays of ashes lay on the floor, on either side of you, and your hands are propped, palms up, suspended by the oven door. Long, delicate fingers point back to the counter opposite.

And there, beside two full jars—the empty, gaping jaws of the Cookie Monster.

Pray, love, forgive me. I'm holding your ashes in it right now.

THE KILLING JAR

My name is Chouko ("butterfly girl") Takeda, and I was born on August 29th, 1967, in a little town called Slocan, BC, just outside of where the old Japanese internment camp used to be. Even when released, my father, Jiro ("second son") remained in that small community because there was still work he could do. He could still teach the children Japanese and Japanese culture. What was left of it, anyway.

I say my father, not because my mother wasn't living at the time, but because she might as well not have been. She was a shadow, trailing along after him, seeking to meet his every need. She rarely spoke, and when she did, it was in hushed tones that were impossible to hear if I was not the one right next to her. She crept like water throughout the home, with soft, fluid footsteps that placed her inches from me sometimes before I was even aware she was there.

I learned little of relationships from my parents, but I know now that even if they spoke fully in front of me, it wouldn't have mattered much.

It seemed that my father was always at school—repairing furniture, planning lessons, gathering wood for the stoves whose fires would have to last through a long, cold winter. All he did at home was eat and sleep and order Mother around. Until the year when I was 7.

That's when he started beating her.

HER LEFT EYE

is black, not blue, from the smack of his hand—is scanning the black of her room—is soft where a hard socket should be—and if she presses hard, tears snake out—is hard to look at straight on—is the pain made plain for all to see, even if she can't—is a cold stare in a warm room, the bite of frost and the reek of flesh burning —is open to the man with the hand—is closed to the man with the hand—is locked away and shut up—kept from desperate scribbles that ask for forgiveness—is the hurt when all he

wants is a second chance, and every
part of her, even the eye, *that* eye,
wants to say,
God, yes!

And on and on it went, a hurricane of slaps, then apologies after. An earthquake of emotions, in him, in me, almost never in *her*—at least it seemed that way. He was frustrated with his students' lack of progress. He was frustrated with their apathy, with their willingness to see their culture fade away. He was frustrated with what had become a tiny life in a tiny space in a corner of the globe most Japanese knew nothing about. He thundered about it all behind closed doors, crashing in on the two of us with more and more power, letting us both slip farther and farther away in his wake.

I found ways to escape.

When a jacket of mine was too threadbare to patch up anymore, I cut the hood off carefully, pulled the drawstring out of it, and threaded through the wire of a coat hanger I'd untwisted. I used a kitchen knife, and then the wire itself to bore two holes into the end of a thick, straight branch I'd found in the bush. Finally, I jammed both ends into it, and wrapped the whole thing with twine —too much twine, really. But I had my butterfly net. And when things turned ugly at home, I sought beauty in other places.

At first, it was just the white, powdery, cabbage butterflies around our garden. Father would pay me for every twenty that I brought him. I think it was his way of making sure I'd stay away for a long, long time.

It wasn't much money, but I would save every bit of it in my secret space—a knothole in a tree near our house. I'd carved it out to make it neater and deeper, so that the money would not be visible to anyone who happened to be walking by. My thin arm could reach down inside, but I never really counted the coins much. I didn't want anyone to know they were there. So I slipped the change inside when I knew no parents were around, no other children were there to see. What I was saving for, I didn't know.

And as I was catching the small white troublemakers, my eyes of course took in the spectrum of other colours flying about me too. Sometimes I forgot what I was doing and just stared as a lovely viceroy (they look like monarchs!) or yellowtail settled on a leaf nearby and spread open its wings slowly, warming them in the sun. I wanted them with me always, not just in quick, fleeting moments that may or may not happen when I needed them most.

It was simple enough. I snuck peeks at one of my father's science texts when he wasn't around. The article *How to Make a Killing Jar* was exactly what I was looking for. *First, obtain a clear jar with a lid that seals tightly.* One of Mom's canning jars. Would she miss it? Probably. Would she mention it to Father? Unlikely. It would only lead to more screaming.

Second, cover it with clear tape so that if it shatters, it won't break. That would take a lot of tape. There was no way I could get that much tape all at once without someone noticing. But bit by bit, at school, I'd snitch small lines of it. After about a month, it was completely covered.

Put some plaster-of-paris in the bottom of the jar, and allow it to harden. This was easier to get than tape. A box of it sat with the few art supplies kept in a cupboard at school. There wasn't enough for an entire class to use, so mostly, this box went unnoticed. I made a paper cone funnel and filled my pockets with as much as I thought I would need. I made sure to do it on a dry day when there was no chance of it mixing in my clothing and making a mess on the way home.

Add a few drops of ethyl acetate and a square of tissue to the jar, and seal it. Ethyl acetate? At first, I had no clue of what it was. I only knew there was likely no chance of finding that kind of chemical out in bush country like Slocan. But then I read that it was used in perfumes, and it evaporated from them quickly, leaving the scent on the skin.

Mother had no perfume at all, so whenever we visited wealthier friends, I made sure to have an eyedropper with me. I'd wait until the adults were deep in conversation, and then I'd go wandering around, eyes wide open for a precious bottle I might quickly suck a bit from. I told myself I wasn't stealing. I was a butterfly child, sucking up sweet nectar from a flower, and then darting off before some angry bird might see me.

It worked too, except the one time that it didn't.

My mother's friend got up to see where I had gone, and she saw me taking the precious fluid from her. When I turned around and saw her staring at me, I dropped the dropper. She walked towards me, picked it up, and placed it in my hand. Then she whispered, “Chouko? Butterfly? Getting to that age? Wanting to feel like an older girl?” She picked up the bottle of perfume and gave it to me. “It’ll be our little secret. Just don’t wear it around your parents. Wash it off before you get home each time.” And she left the room. I had an entire bottle of the precious fluid to myself, and I kept it in the tree with my coins.

My killing jar was complete, and I had to hide it too, of course. I burrowed out a hole under a bush to place it safely out of harm’s way. When I needed it, I’d bring the butterfly, drop it inside, and the vapours would kill it quickly, making it possible for me to open and pin the wings gently to my bedroom wall. My father thought I was taking an interest in nature, and he was pleased. Not that I would become some scientist of course—that would never happen since I was a girl—but because I had something to keep me occupied and out of his hair.

Mom needs her own killing jar, I thought, but then the fullness of what that might mean struck me, and I wished I’d been able to un-think it. For months, I saw a giant butterfly in my dreams, one with Dad’s face, going blissfully to sleep in a clear glass cage held in my mother’s hands.

In the end, it was much simpler than that.

He simply gathered up all that was important to him and left late, once everyone was sleeping, never speaking a word, a shadow in the night. One shadow slipping away from another. Unseen, unheard. And there *was* help from others, for a while, but eventually, the shame of being beggars to our friends drove Mother and me away. We took flight ourselves, and were drawn to the bright lights of the big city, Vancouver.

What hurt me most of all at the time, though, wasn't Father. It wasn't even Mother's bruises or tears. It was having to leave behind my wall of wings. Before we left, I unpinned my favourite, a large tangerine viceroy, and pressed it carefully between the pages of a book. I also visited the tree and took the coins, but I left the perfume behind.

I would have no use for it in the city.

And the city was where I found my own white troublemakers. Not the cabbage butterfly variety, either. My mother and I were at the market, trying to make our meagre amount of money stretch as far as it could. It seemed as though everywhere we went, we heard it:

JAPANESE INTERNMENT CAMP
Slocan, 1942

Can you see me, now,
I am the chink
the flat face, the
dirty Jap,
who's not at home in
a "friendly" country...

Can you see you, then,
in your armour—I am
glass that mirrors you—
the filthy view *you* present,
what is meant to be
a "friendly" country.

Can you see me, now, can you see you, then,
I am the chink in your armour—I am
the flat face, the glass that mirrors you—
dirty Jap, the filthy view *you* present,
who's not at home in what is meant to be
a "friendly" country...a "friendly" country.

It's a lean world from behind cold walls.
You watch me scratch out my serpent-like stems,
figures in the air no one else can see,
cracks through which rays of light can find their way—

But the wall is sure stone. These are mere words,
yet syllables also rock or enclose.
You have clearly come here to build your walls;

I have clearly come here to tear them down.

Public Market
Vancouver, 1982

You have to understand. I'd only ever been around Japanese, at least as far back as I could remember. And at Slocan, we all knew our place and were aiming to improve, knowing all the while it'd be an uphill battle, especially when anti-Japanese sentiments were still running high decades after the attack on Pearl Harbour. But mostly, in Slocan, there were other people around me who were just like me. *Here*, I was the face in the crowd who didn't belong.

Bad enough, but to hear comments like "Ya bloody Chink! Get out of my way and go back to where you came from!" was all too much. I had no response, no coping strategies to call on—no butterflies, butterfly nets, or killing jars to put things to sleep in these city streets.

And it was then I turned to pen and paper. It was easy enough to find things to write on and things to write with, without having to pay for them. Little stubby pencils at the stand outside the golf course. The backs of notices tacked up on public bulletin boards—clean and tidy and waiting for words. And of course, I could fit an entire poem on the back of a single sheet, so, more for a desire of length and less than any other quality, poetry became my escape.

Any time I saw an orange sheet posted, I got excited. I could draw a large viceroy butterfly on the back of it, press hard with my pencil to make the dark outlines of the wings, and later, tear carefully around the edges. In this way, I kept the delicate creatures with me even when I was walking down hard city streets. The butterflies were me—sweet, delicate, and beautiful, for the most part, but rough around the edges too.

My butterflies could live on in my poems, doing what would be impossible in the real world. They could grow into giants, lift off and carry that log wall to the sea, drop it in as a raft that could flow with the currents to explore the world beyond, lifting warm wing sails, filling emptiness with a wind rushing in, cruising far off into the ocean, to the islands beyond.

But right now, those rude white boys were following me, pointing at me, and I was hurrying away as fast as I could, darting between the stalls, doing my best to lose them, doing my best to find my mother. My tiny frame flitted between the other adults easily, but in my panic to get away, and in the sea of legs all around me, I soon lost sight of where I was and where I was headed.

And then all at once the bodies seemed to part, and I saw her, crouching on the sidewalk, her back against a brick wall. Not my mother, but the girl I would come to know as Yee-Fun.

YEE-FUN, MAIN & HASTINGS

Under a broken sky,
the day dark and gloomy with light,
she casts a skinny shadow,
drives life into a corner,
shelters herself in a temporary
booth of boards,
the darkness
rising, the melancholy
fate of the place exploding
in a cave of echoes

Her heart holds
remnants of hiding
places, secret rooms
and hidden tunnels,
but few accounts
of what *really* happened—

No one wants to know.

So she keeps quiet and has nightmares,
daymares, life-and-death struggles,
herself a slave of circumstance,
stubbornness, cruelty, failings

She flees with whatever she can take,
escaping
the buildings
that flow around her

Innocence begins to crack.

Driven by anger and hatred,
and the revenge she so desperately seeks,
she walks out of her life,
and when she comes to die,
she discovers that she has not lived—
no last name for a gravestone, just

Yee-fun, Main & Hastings.

Okay, a bit melodramatic maybe. The girl *was* alive, after all. But she was the closest thing I'd ever seen to a corpse in all my life, and I just *had* to write about her later on. She was skin and bones, and I could practically count her ribs through the washed-out yellow shirt she wore.

Sunken eyes, pale skin, and an apathetic expression that seemed lost in some faraway world. But as soon as the first hand gripped my shoulder from behind, she sprang into action.

She jammed her fingertips straight into the throat of the first boy, and kicked another beside him as hard as she could in the crotch. Both boys dropped to their knees immediately, and she just stared at the third, holding her hands on her hips. He backed up a few steps and then the other two rose to their feet and turned around as well. “Fuckin’ street slime!” one muttered under his breath. “Yellow bitch!” said another.

And it was then that I saw her smile the most beautiful smile. It spread across her face and lit up her eyes as she slowly shook her head from side to side. “Jap girl, you have V for Victim stamped on that forehead of yours. If you’re going to survive, you’re going to have to get a lot tougher. Like this.” She pulled a 1945 nickel from her pocket and showed me the giant V on the front of it. “This coin is hard, with edges, and the V on *it* means Victory. Get it?” She left the coin in my hand and curled my fingers around it, showing me that I was to keep it.

She? Had helped *me*? With a V. For Victory. Or Vancouver. Or Viceroy. I slipped the coin into my pocket, and kept my hand there, looking down, stammering out a “Th-thank you.”

“Hold out your hand.”

I thought she meant to shake it, but when I held it out to do so, she grabbed it, turned it so that it was horizontal, not vertical. “Like this. Hard and together. And you aim for the throat. Now try it on me, on my stomach."

When I hesitated, she grabbed my wrist and pulled it to her, jamming my fingers against what little flesh there was of her.

And that's when another hand gripped my shoulder from behind—my mother's. "We have to go now," she whispered, and started firmly steering me away.

I glanced over my shoulder. "Chouko," I said. It was all I could get out.

"Yee-fun," I heard back. And that's the unlikely way I would meet my best friend in the world.

As I walked away with Mother, I slid my hand back into my pocket. Over and over again, my fingertip traced the outline of the V. That shape, like butterfly wings opening wide. I flipped it over and pressed it hard against my thigh. I was determined to make it part of me.

Money lasted a long, long time in bush country, where people traded vegetables from their own garden for meat from the latest hunting trip or a jar of canned fruit from someone's root cellar. And it wasn't a case of so much of this for one of that—you just traded some of what you had extra for some of what you needed.

But in the city, everything costs money, not zucchini.

Right from the beginning, Mother knew that we needed to put our money into food, not shelter, because we didn't have much while she was trying to find work.

Even then, the money ran out and she was still unemployed. Anti-Japanese sentiments were still strong. I won't call it outright racism, just unfair suspicion. But it was enough to keep us hungry and on the streets.

Yee-fun, of course, came to my rescue again.

"Well, if you like, you can stay with me. But only you, not your mother."

"How come?"

"Look, Victory Girl, you're sweet and all, but haven't you ever wondered about how I eat? About how I afford a place to stay? It sure isn't delivering newspapers."

I could feel my face flushing red. "You mean you—"

"Suck a cock or two? Yes, I do. And it means nothing to me. And it gives others what they want. And that gives me what I want—money to survive."

She glared at me like *I* was the one doing something wrong. But when she saw that I wasn't about to judge, her look softened. She placed both her hands on my cheeks and raised my head to look at her. "Look, Victory—Vicki—I know *that* life's not for you, and I can probably even help you out for a while. But I sometimes bring clients here, you know? It'd be kind of awkward for your mother to see and hear me having sex with strangers all the time."

And just like that, she'd given me a new home and a new name.

THE PERSON I'M NOT

She began
as an enigma,
a sliver of a shadow,

but now she rolls
into my bones,
builds ghostly genes

with ease, fleshes
out forms, and sculpts
onto my skeleton

with a grating patience
that waits like a black
cat cancer

The tendons tug,
just a whisker twitch
at first, but then I feel

the full stretch,
the tightening
along my spine,

vertebrae falling
into line, like the tail
of a kite—

She can reel
me in now anytime
she wants, play

me like a puppet,
a fish on a line—
more strings.

The movements
are stiff, robotic
at first, a pubescent

problem with an adult
mind, and I find,
over time, ways to round

out those corners, strum
lines of an hourglass guitar—
More strings,

but these sing,
swing me from
conscious thought,

from a droning tone
that's whispering
a warning to me,

a voice, a monotone
I know as my own,
but I want to believe

I'm in charge,
that there's no remote
control of my soul,

so I ignore the pull,
renounce all gods,
cut the strings,

think things
for myself.
The lines entwine,

trip me up, wrap
around a body
that's out of control,

and I face
the pavement, smack
hard against the truth

that's plain to see
as I cry out "My God!"
against the pain,

and I realize that faith remains,
filling in the sliver
of a shadow

of a person I'm not.

I certainly didn't feel victorious. I mean, I had shelter for myself now, but what was my mother supposed to do? Yee-fun told me it would be easier if I wasn't with her, bogging her down. And that's what I told Mother later that evening.

"Chouko, you don't have to do this." My mother was already crying. I could tell it was because she felt that *she* had failed me. Failed to give me the life she thought I deserved. And while Yee-fun wasn't her favourite person in the world, I think she knew that if I could find food and shelter, it would make it easier for her to do the same.

She held my face in her hands the same way Yee-fun had earlier. "Only for a short time. Only until I find work. Once I do, you come back to live with your mother, yes?"

"Yes." That was what I said. But deep down, I think we both knew it might never happen. Rent was expensive. Food was expensive. And we had less than nothing. Not even our pride remained. Both broken. The powder rubbed from our wings.

I wandered the streets alone for a long, long time that first day. Everywhere I went, I looked for *those* women, the ones with high heels and the cheap makeup. I couldn't help but think of Yee-fun. How could she be so good and so bad at the same time?

I began to wonder if some of these other "evil" people around me might have good qualities of their own too. And that's when I spotted her—a prostitute who could've been my mother's age:

STREET TALKER

There's music in the way she moves,
sleek stilettos striking sidewalks,
pulling rhythms from rock and stone,
street sounds beckoning from below,

long legs spreading out the syllables,
blocking out the beats, notes lingering
in the crowd, a slow pulse lagging
at the curb, pulling me close,

and as she gets the green light
that waves her away, I lose
her in a storm of suits and ties,
her body melting into the masses,

blending into buildings that seek
to shadow her sound. But that song
remains, pulling me down straight
lines that hold the notes together

She plays black shoe blues for me,
cruises around a corner
while I hold my course. The streets
can steal her from me, drift

her down some nowhere alley
to some nothing place, swallow
her whole, take away dignity
and pride—but never that song

There's music in the way she moves.

How would I feel one day, if I was walking the streets, and saw my mother doing this work? Was this the price of freedom?

Even as I told myself that it was something she would never do, something I would never do, I knew it was a lie. People did what they had to in order to survive. And I looked at these streets again with fresh eyes.

I would stay with Yee-fun. Maybe the two of us could find a new life together. Maybe I could help her the way that she was helping me. As far as I could tell, she had no butterfly dreams of her own. I would lend her mine, as payment for her kindness.

I rounded the corner at Main and Hastings, close to where we'd first met. I found the alleyway entrance with the stairs to her apartment, but just as I was about to knock, I stopped. I heard crying inside.

The door wasn't even locked. I tried the handle, pushed the door gently in. "Yee-fun?"

"Go! Go away, Vicki. I don't want you to—"

I stepped fully into the room and saw her cowering in a corner, all bloody and bruised.

"—see me this way. Fucking jerk! He, he hurt me...bad. And he found where I kept my rent money too. He took everything, Vicki. Everything."

I just held her in my arms. I didn't know what to say, didn't think anything I said would matter to her at a time like this. I felt stupid with the next words I heard tumbling from my lips: "Is, is anything broken? Do you need a doctor?"

She said nothing, but just melted into me. I could feel her heartbeat racing the way mine was too. I did my best to suck in long, slow breaths—to breathe them out the same way. Eventually, my pulse slowed, and after a long time, I felt her heartbeat match my own, felt her breathing take on the same rhythm.

I helped her to the bed. The sheet was already stained, so I didn't worry about making it worse. I found a cloth and ran some warm water, slowly sponging away the blood. I treated the scratches on her face, her back as best I knew how. And then I just lay down beside her, giving her the only comfort I could. As soon as she was sleeping, I reached over to the night table, grabbed my science text, and slipped a large paper butterfly from between its pages. I tucked it between her fingers so that it would be the first thing she saw when she woke up.

Thankfully, it would be many years before I encountered anything that would make me feel like that again. By the time I reached what was then almost my mother's age, I did though—the rapes that happened in the aftermath of Hurricane Katrina:

KATRINA'S HURRICANE

I saw the signs, I could tell the **Storms**
were close. "Come, now, hurry,"—and **I feel**
myself pushed down basement stairs, to a **tiny**
room. I don't have to wait long. Violent **attacks**
that keep me pinned—the wind, icy **fingers**
clutch and **grab**
for **any**
opening
A single, shuttered **window**
that lets in no light—now **burst**
through, cloth **torn**
as the **violence**
finds its way **inside**
Shards cut **deep**
and blood runs. These **wounds**
will later become visible **scars**—
the same scars I see on my **wrists**

as I reach to shut off the **life**
support of the only **man**
who has ever **touched me**
that way
There was no **hurricane**
He was my **hurricane**
Now see **again**
with fresh eyes, and **you'll know**
my pain.

Storms. I feel tiny attacks. Fingers grab any opening, window burst, torn violence inside, deep wounds, scars—wrists, life. Man touched me that way. Hurricane, hurricane, again you'll know my pain.

It's what I felt the day I found Yee-fun bruised and bloodied, a day when I still did not fully understand the word "rape." It's what made me cry as I read the accounts of girls stranded, accepting the help of strangers, only to be taken somewhere and gang-raped. It's what I felt the day Yee-fun died.

Now I know what you're thinking, and what you need to know. What about the gaps in between, that long sidewalk crack that seems to go on forever?

Well, yes, it's filled with dirt and grime.

And no, my mother's story is not a happy ending.

But although Yee-fun and my mother never did make it to an old age, I will. And I still find pleasure in my poetry, but now, there's something more. I'm standing in a fabric store on Commercial Drive, right now, one that I own—I always *did* have an eye for pretty things—and I'm setting up for the day.

Watch me as I cut off a diaphanous piece of orange chiffon and drape it around my shoulders.

Come with me as I walk outside in the morning breeze.

It's five a.m., not a soul outside my store. And I stretch that cloth from arm to arm behind me—Vicki, with a V, Chouko, the viceroy girl—and I open my wings to the wind…

and then fold them and rub my rounded belly to let you know I'm here. I take out the nickel, the one with the V, and press it gently against you. One day, you will feel this freedom too.

CHRYSALIS

The sun rolls away **again,**
and in its place are **shifting**
shadows, black bones **sliding**
across my **skin,**
the music **melting**
over **me**

I'm **pinned**
by stone **wings**
by kisses **camouflaged**
as love—my breath **held hostage**
like smoke in my throat

This is how you **sculpt freedom**
not **into something,**
but **from something,**
the cocoon

breaking up

PLOW BREAKS SOIL

Mick learned, way back in '43, that there was nothing simple about the simple folk of Riverview Gap. He himself had New Year's for a birthday, a horse—Horizon—for a pet, and a corpse for a father. His pa, "Uncle Willie" to most everyone, himself included, was laid up ages ago, the result of some stroke that had paralyzed him top to bottom. That left Mick's ma, "Aunt Nell," to tend to a sprawling 97-acre hill farm in the boonies, along with five kids, and, of course, Uncle Willie.

At first, she did it all and did it well, but when her right ankle stiffened up on her and never quite made its way back to normal, the farm started to show the strain. A walk into the barn was all it ever took to remind Mick how, over time, animals and objects could fall into damage and disrepair—livestock skin and bones, tractor seats rusted, stalls that needed mucking, machinery busted, and all of it multiplyin' like the McKinley family of seventeen, their closest neighbours, a twenty-minute drive away.

Over time, Mick saw how rust and dust, pig slop and cow manure, broken this and rotted that could slip on out of the barn and into their lives.

He didn't want a speck of it.

He wanted to ditch the farm and head over to some little town, one with more than a few people in it. Girls, especially. He'd find work in salt mines or coal mines or in nearby fields or wherever they needed young muscles and strong backs, and he'd make his way—away from here.

No kids. Just a wife and a life and time left to enjoy it all.

And that dream lasted right up until the year he'd turn 19.

He was relaxing in a recliner in the sitting room when the doc came by to tell them about Aunt Nell's test results.

"Tumour's bigger'n expected. Don't think I'd be makin' plans past Christmas." And he said it right in front of her like she was some lame horse that would have to be put down.

Nell just looked him straight in the eye, no tears, no nothin', and said, "Plow breaks soil so seeds can grow."

And then she looked straight at Mick.

He ducked his hands into his pockets and stared at the floor like it was the most interesting dirt he'd ever seen. Then he backed on out of that room and headed for the hayloft.

He didn't make it nearly that far. Not ten yards out of

the house, he heard the groan, a long slow moan that sounded like an engine out of oil, right before it catches fire. Heifer layin' on her side. Nell and Willie inside. And the other kids too young to be useful. It was up to him.

Mick went to the barn, slid the door to the side, and lifted a noose of rope from a hook nearby. Then he made his way back to the mother cow. "She's not asleep and dreamin', that's for sure." And he knelt on her back legs, pinning them to the ground, and he grabbed the rope and pushed it deep inside, real deep, elbow deep, looping it around the baby's hocks inside the mother. Once it was good and tight, he stood, keeping his foot planted firmly on the back legs of the mother.

For what seemed like forever, he yanked and tugged, pulling up and over and back, and the legs of the calf popped out the backside and he grabbed onto both of them and slid that calf out slick as a whistle.

The calf was fine. Nothin' broken or bleedin'. But the mother was a mess.

The heifer was bleedin' out somethin' bad, and she wasn't moving anymore. He took the rope off the calf and watched the baby take a drunken walk over to its ma. Then he turned away as the young one began sucking milk from the udder of a dead mother.

Mick's own ma was starin' straight at him now too, hands on hips, a huge smile on her face. "I know it's hard, real hard," she said, wiping her hands on her apron like *she'd* just delivered the calf or somethin'.

"Plow breaks soil so seeds can grow."

And that was that. He'd proven himself useful, so

this'd be his life. Forever. With four littluns and an invalid to care for on top of it all. And he'd be an adult and all by then, so he'd be expected to grow up super-fast.

Don't think I'd be makin' plans past Christmas.

So he treaded the long way out to the west field to mend some fences, and just after he'd tacked the barbed wire back to the first post, he turned around and Nell was there.

He took a step back, tripped and stopped his fall by grabbing a handful of barbs. When he stood and pulled his hand away, blood streamed down his wrist somethin' awful, just like that dead heifer.

And Nell looked at him and said, "Plow breaks soil so seeds can grow." And she limped away at such a snail's pace that Mick wondered how she'd ever managed to get out there so quickly in the first place.

All night, his dreams were mighty disturbed, and in the last one before he woke, he was kneeling hard on the heifer's hind legs, reaching deep inside the cow, and she was bawlin' and he was screamin' and blood was coursin' out, and when he jerked his hand clear, he was holdin' a giant ball of barbed wire, and it was tangled all around his fist, and it snaked up his arm, and over his shoulder, and then it began to tighten around his neck. And he was gasping for air, pushing and pulling—

and that's when he woke up. And he was kneeling on Nell, and he had a pillow pushed tight across her face. And she wasn't movin'.

And he had no tears, no nothin' and he said, "Plow breaks soil so seeds can grow."

And that's when little 6-year-old Lizzie walked in.

And as calm as could be, he told her, "Aunt Nell's not well. I need your help. Can you go get somethin' for me?" And she nodded slowly, and he said, "That noose of rope hangin' on the hook near the barn door? You know the one?"

And she nodded again and headed out the door in her nightgown and bare feet.

And he knew Nell's body would explain itself away, what with the tumour and all. But Lizzie's would be a tougher tale. Would there be an accident, or would he make certain her body would never be found?

At least her trip to fetch the rope would buy him time to think. A gunnysack of rocks, like what they did with unwanted farm cats is what he decided on. That deep marsh, the one overgrown with weeds, the one no one in his right mind fished in anymore.

And with tragedy hurtlin' around him like a hurricane, who'd expect anything of a boy who wasn't even an adult yet?

And just like that, the winds calmed, the skies cleared, and Mick began making plans for well past Christmas.

"Plow breaks soil," he said, and he leaned over to the other side of the bed and placed the pillow over his father's face.

THE HIGH PRICE OF FISH

They were father, husband, brother, son. They were known as the finest kind. Their lives and their loss have touched our community in profound ways. We remain strengthened by their character, inspired by their courage and proud to call them Gloucestermen.

Angelica wasn't so sure. One thing *was* certain—they were all dead, all 5,368 of them. And those were just the names listed here on these plaques—there were likely double that number. Heavy numbers for a city of 30,000. Like Civil War heavy. Like World War I and II heavy. But these were fishermen, not soldiers.

Fishermen.

She stepped back to take a good look at the *Man at the Wheel* memorial. Big bronze statue of a bearded fisherman wearing the local uniform—oilskins and a sou'wester. His fingers clenched the ship's wheel tightly as he gazed across the harbour to open waters beyond. Below him, carved into the pedestal he stood on: *They that go down to the sea in ships*. What was that all about anyway? Just what was the attraction? Here she was, engaged to a fisherman, and she still couldn't—

"Whaddya, retahded?"

Speak of the devil. Angelica turned quickly, hands on her hips. "You talking to me, Boston Boy?"

"I am, I am. Didn't mean you no harm. Just saw your eyes wide as a dieter's ass is all."

"Eloquent as ever." She walked right up to him, hugged him hard, then looked up into his dark eyes. "Remind me what I see in you?"

He leaned down and whispered: "I would, but I'd get arrested for indecent exposhah."

She hated it when he played up the accent. "Ah, yes, now I remember." She gave him a quick peck on the cheek, stepped back, and stared long and hard at his crotch. "Your sense of humour."

"Ouch. The lady's got teeth like a barracuda."

"If you're not careful, they just might eat you up."

He grabbed her hand and pulled her quickly to him, kissed her hard. "That's a risk I'll take any day." He glanced in the same direction as the statue. "Ready to check out what a day in my life is like?"

She rolled her eyes. "Not exactly, but let's get it done and over with. I suppose I should know how you spend those long hours away from me." What she really wanted was an idea of how long such a trip could really take, and why. Not that she was trying to make him account for all those hours away, but it was always good to do your research. Especially if there could be another woman involved.

They walked slowly down the pier, arm in arm. She was shocked when she saw the boat. "You're—I mean, you did it already? You're wonderful!"

"Yeh," he said, staring at his sandals. "Yeh."

She'd recently convinced him to paint over the name —"Crystal," and she was certainly no Crystal—so now it read *Isle of View*, and the dinghy it towed read *Isle of View II*. It was cutesy, she knew, and he'd likely catch hell for it from all his fisher buddies, but it was her little test after all. Just how serious *was* he about her? To her surprise, he'd made the change immediately. She didn't even have to nag once.

He loved her, he really did. Didn't he?

As they climbed aboard, she scrunched her nose at the bumper stickers plastered on the wheelhouse:

A skull and crossbones with "Surrender the Booty" under it.

A red and white one that read "I brake for tuna."

And a third with "Save a tuna—eat a dolphin!"

"You do know those will have to be stripped and cleaned and sent to someone special, yes?"

"And who might you have in mind?"

"Crystal." She smirked, but Crystal was still a sore spot for her—like a barnacle hanging on, refusing to let go. No doubt Blake still had feelings for that woman.

"I'll get right on that." He picked a large hook from a tackle box, used it to pick at the corners of the stickers, then ripped each one off by pulling sharply from both ends at the same time. The bumper stickers popped off cleanly—along with a fair amount of paint. The colour underneath was white, but the surrounding hue was sky blue. It didn't match at all. Blake looked at Angelica and laughed at her pained expression. "I like it—I like it a lot. It's like a bit of that abstract art we saw last weekend—well, that art you handcuffed me to for a few hours or so."

He was trying too hard, she thought. Hiding something?

Just as he was about to cast off the lines, he spotted Don Wilson, a 79-year-old Gloucester native walking past on the pier.

"Hey, old man!"

"Hey Blake! Howareya? You hear the one about the difference between a guitar and a fish?"

"No, what's the difference?"

"You can't tune a fish."

Blake laughed loudly. "Whaddya mean, old man? I tuna fish every day of my life almost."

The old man waved him close, and whispered, just a bit too loudly: "Bad luck to take a woman on board. The ship's yer lady, don'tcha know? Don't want yer boat to get jealous now, do ya?"

Blake could feel Angelica getting closer. "Of course we'll take care, old man. No need to worry about the two of us."

As they pulled away from shore, Angelica put her

hands on Blake's cheeks and turned his head so he was looking straight at her. "Now what was that whispering all about?"

"What? Don? He's like the dad I never had. Just lookin' out for his boy is all. Can you believe he tells me that same joke most every time we meet? And I just pretend it's the very first time I've heard it, just so he can have his fun."

Okay, she thought. Not an outright lie at least. Sparing her feelings, maybe? That old man didn't even know her. Superstitious old coot. What right did he—

"Figured I'd show you why tuna fishing is *hahd.* Wicked *hahd.* And we'd best be gettin' goin' 'specially since this weekend is a holiday. Goddamn Googans'll be all over the place like sea rats, this bein' a holiday weekend and all."

Her turn to laugh. "Googans? Sea rats? Sounds like Harry Potter or something. Would you mind speaking English for five minutes for this landlubber lady, please?"

Blake opened up a lid on what appeared to be a gigantic ice chest. "Googans. Tourists and weekend warriors who get in the way and eat into the catch of commercial fishermen like me. Sea rats—seagulls that can swoop down and eat fish or scoop up all your chum."

"Scoop up your chums? This *is* Harry Potter—gigantic seagulls diving from the sky and carrying us all off?"

He pulled a bucket of what appeared to be diced-up fish out of the ice chest. "Chum of another kind. You'll find out. In fact, I'll even put you in charge of the chum." He handed the bucket to her, and she held it as far away from herself as she could.

"Smelly bunch of chums you fisherman keep around."

"Awww, you're not so bad, Angel."

She swatted him lightly with her free hand. "So what do I do with the bucket?"

"Well," he said, "that's an easy job, but an important one. When we get to our fishin' spot, you need to slowly dump that in the water as we cruise along a bit. Attract the fish to us, instead of goin' to chase them. We'll discuss the *second* bucket when we get there."

"So let me get this straight," she said, putting the pail down. "You use fish to catch fish? Doesn't that kind of defeat the purpose?"

"Takes money to make money, right? Somethin' like that."

He went into the wheelhouse and gunned the engine. Once they were out on the open waters, he explained some more. "Chum come in handy two ways. First, we toss a bucket or two overboard, like I said. Second, we bait hooks with 'em too." He smiled a wicked smile.

"But I thought you used—like nets, that type of thing."

"Some do. I mean, I can't afford a big trawler or anything yet myself. But if I can land a few good ones, I'll be set."

"A few fish are going to help you pay for a boat? Now that's a fish tale if ever I've heard one. What are you going to do next, tell me about the big one that got away?" She thought of Crystal as soon as the words escaped her lips. Damn.

"These aren't just salmon or somethin', you know? A

good Bluefin can fetch $20,000 in the right market."

"$20,000 for a—for a fish?"

"Well, it's right hard to catch a quality one like that though. But yes, it's possible, and I'll bet that would buy even someone with your fancy tastes a pair of shoes or two."

"Just a few," she answered, shaking her head. "I still can't believe there are people willing to pay that much."

"When you want something bad enough," he said, pulling her close again, "you'll pay the price. Even name your boat *Isle of View* and stuff like that."

"And *Isle of View II*," she replied. "See how perfectly that works?"

"Cute won't catch the tuna. We need baited hooks for that. Sure you're up for the job?"

"I hope you have gloves for me. I just got my nails done."

He said nothing, just kept slapping his leg, laughing.

"I'll take that as a no. Well, I might as well help anyway. There's nothing else to do out here, and if I help, we'll be out of here twice as fast, yes?"

"True as the north star," he said, picking up a hook and a piece of chum. "Of course, I hope we're home before it's dark enough to see it...."

She grabbed a hook herself and mirrored his movements. For a long time, her bait kept slipping off the hooks as soon as they hit the water, but after a while, she got the hang of it. Fresh air, a cruise on the open water with her fiancé—not so bad after all.

"You're baitin' those hooks so good right now,"

Blake said, peering over her shoulder, "that I think congratulations are in order. As captain of this ship, I give you the official name of Master Baiter."

She groaned and rolled her eyes. "You've been waiting a long time to use that one, haven't you?"

"Better to see it in action than just to name it," he said, raising and lowering his eyebrows rapidly.

"You pervert. I love you."

"But not as much as you love bein' a Master Baiter, yeah?" He started laughing uncontrollably again.

Oh well, let him have his fun. At least he was having his fun *with* her, and not without her. Maybe that was the real reason she agreed to this. Was she worried he might take Crystal out with him if she refused? That was ridiculous. Crystal was over and done with. She had to convince herself of that or she'd drive herself mad.

And just like that, it seemed like someone turned the lights out. The clouds had come in crazy quickly, and the wind and waves were picking up. She didn't want to look like the stereotypical weak female, but—

"Well, you've given it a try. I think we can call it a day."

Blake was giving up...before her? She was sure he was doing it for her, but right now, she didn't care.

"I'll start packing things up since I know where everything goes. You okay with reeling in the lines?"

"Sure am," she said, grabbing the closest rod from its holder. "Especially if it's going to make me a fisherwoman instead of a Mas—"

Zing! Just like that, a fish hit the hook and hit it hard! It nearly jerked her overboard, and she threw all her weight backwards to fight it. She took her hand off the reel and line started spinning out quickly. If it snapped, she'd land smack on her back, but it was all she could do until Blake got a hand on the rod too.

Blake put the drag on heavier, then started reeling in some of the line. "Got to keep it tight," he said. "No slack or the fish'll dive and wrap it around somethin', snap it like a twig." The line slackened a lot all of a sudden, and he thought it must have snapped, but then he saw why there was so much for him to reel in—the fish surfaced right next to the boat, then dove down again.

It was the largest fish Angelica had ever seen in person. "You mean, *that's* what you're fishing for?"

"Nah, I'm not fishing for that," Blake said, feeling the line go tight again, feeling the rod bend near double. "I'm fishing for the cost of our wedding, the best one ever."

She saw him lean back and pull hard. He would do it, he would land this fish, if only his strength held out.

"Do me a favour?" he asked. "Fish gloves—green rubber ones in the wheelhouse, on the counter. Get them for me? My hands are a bit raw."

She stopped and looked at him. "You mean, you had gloves all along? And there I was, getting my hands all fishy—"

"Hurry, will ya? My fingers are getting raw!"

She ran into the wheelhouse, and she saw the gloves right away, on the floor in front of her, but she saw something else too. The waves had rocked another item loose from who knows where it was hidden. A book with photos and notes pasted into it, and there, on the floor, was Crystal's photo smiling up at her, mocking her.

"Angelica!"

Hearing her own name, from Blake, and seeing this picture, one kept by Blake, kept from her by Blake, and who knows how many other secrets—something just kind of snapped inside. She ran out with the gloves, raced to him, actually, and lost her footing, slamming into his back hard, sending him reeling over the edge into the waves. She saw him go under, and she never saw him come up again.

The next thing she knew, there were two people at her side, saying her name over and over again. A nurse and... Don Wilson?

"Lucky Mr. Wilson got worried and came looking for you. You're going to be all right, Miss. You're going to be all right."

Angelica looked up at her. "And Blake? Where's Blake? He saved Blake too, didn't he? Didn't he?"

Don muttered something under his breath that she could have sworn was "Women on a ship. I told him about women on a ship." He gave her the nastiest look he could muster, and as he walked over to a police officer, she saw him hand something over to him. The book. The Crystal book.

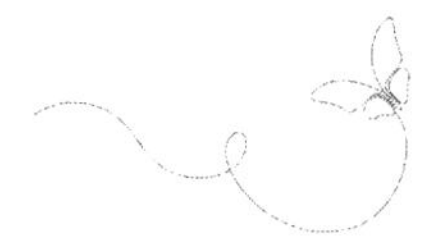

Turns out that there was something tucked into the back cover of that book. A little letter from Blake's lawyer:

"Here's your copy of the policy with the changed beneficiary. Let me know if there is anything else I can help you with."

They read it out in court, and now, she couldn't get it out of her head. Her name—on the life insurance papers, and the names of the boats too—*Isle of View* and *Isle of View II*. It was clear what it all must look like to the others. Crystal clear. But she hadn't meant to—had she? Even she didn't know.

Don Wilson sat in the back of the court room staring hard at the nape of her neck. He didn't have a reason to hate the new girl, did he? But Blake was dead, and he'd been through tougher storms than this and scraped through just fine in the past. Hell, even a retired 79-year-old had navigated through that speck of a squall, hadn't he? The girl had to be to blame. And now he had a reason that made sense to everyone and their dog.

But of course, it wasn't all that easy. And of course, Don had his own secret too. When they'd dredged the bottom to find the body, police reported that they had found the rod and reel "tangled up" with the body of the dead man. What they didn't report was what Don had seen with his own two eyes.

Blake's fingers were still gripping that damn pole.

BUILD IT UP RIGHT

My fiancée is a bodybuilder, if you know what I mean. She gets the way things are, versus the way people say they are. I mean, that whole *Don't judge a book by its cover* thing is a pile of shit. The average asshole is swayed by appearance all the time, and that keeps my slender salad-eating, Barbie-smiling blondie busy all day long.

She builds her body.

Not with weights or circuit training or anything like that—no, that's more my thing—though she *can* get hot and sweaty when she wants to, if you know what I mean. No, she builds with her own materials—makeup, like mascara and foundation and lipstick and eye shadow, and padded bras and plastic surgery, and purses and necklaces, watches and rings, pretty dresses and fancy clothes. She's a real material girl that way. I swear I can hear the cash registers ringing in the background as she snaps quick small steps in stilettos down some sidewalk on Sunset, that *click-clack* tapping out a backbeat as she glides down the street smooth as the silk that shivers down her shoulders to meet those high heels.

It's an effort for her to look that good, and I ought to know since I've been with her for the past eighteen months. And she loves me crazy lots, because I know the secret. Watch her. Praise her. Notice the little things—that new shade of lipstick, the latest highlights from the hairdresser, that outfit she just picked out and picked up from a place that charges way too much for a fistful of cloth. A few words go a long way sometimes. Most of the time. She taught me that too. I mean, really, I could give a shit, but that's the point. Most guys feel that way. So if you're not most guys, you get the girl and all it takes is a bit of effort and it pays off with arm candy that's all tits and teeth and the envy of every guy in the room, including the married ones. Especially the married ones.

And feeling her hand on me—on my hand, my arm, my shoulder—I mean, that comes at a cost for me too, and I don't just mean money. My body has to be muscled and ripped and hard and thick and the envy of all those female friends she seems to scare up here, there, and everywhere. Otherwise, I'm no use to her either.

And I mean, she has a few bucks, like Bill Gates bucks or Donald Trump bucks or the Sultan of Brunei bucks or that-Mexican-guy-whose-name-I-can't-remember-but-who-is-actually-the-richest-dude-in-the-world bucks. I mean, if she did work out, it wouldn't be at *Gold's Gym*—my torture chamber of choice—it'd be at *Golden Gym*, if you know what I mean. I've also learned not to use words like *dude* around her and her friends, and that's actually easier than I thought it would be, because the trick is to say one nice thing about something they're holding or wearing, and then just sit back and let the hen party begin. Take a step back and play the strong, silent type and they'll call you charming and sweet and sensitive for a guy with *your* build, and stuff like that.

Oh yeah, you shouldn't use words like *stuff* or *yeah* either.

In any case, in spite of a rich daddy who thinks he owns her and everything connected to her for life, in spite of no sisters, no brothers, and being the only child, spoiled rotten and all, in spite of a mouse of a mother who cowers in a corner every time Daddy gives her a look, *that* look, in spite of me and my simple background and my barroom brawls and tailgate parties—you know, all those hillbilly ways of me and my bros, I mean the ones by birth and those brothers of other mothers—in spite of all those teeth whitening treatments and Botox injections and silicone implants (are they growing or is it just me?), in spite of all those thousands of jars and bottles and brushes and creams and God knows what on her bathroom counter, my girl loves her lifestyle and wouldn't change anything in it for the world, not even me. Can you believe it?

Well, at least that's how it looks, and that's what Daddy used to think, and it's why we're actually looking for a place together now, just the two of us.

And I mean, my gym rat brothers just don't get it—I mean why someone with looks that'd make God himself cheat on the not-so Virgin Mary is with me and lookin' to be with me for some time. That just gets 'em. And I mean, they're great guys and all—the kinda bros who'd give you the last can outta the two-four, even if they was thirsty as a salt-lickin' desert rat with a throatfulla sand—but I've had to leave them all behind too.

And Becca, well Rebecca, that jaw-dropping fiancée of mine, well, she's left her friends and family behind to be with me, you see? And she's managed to leave them while hanging on to all her money and leaving all her worries behind. And she's got a plan to start over away from all the expectations—the ones that were making her pump Prozac and painkillers and manic-this and depression-that and uppers and downers and in-betweeners, like she was a mile underwater and they was her oxygen tank or somethin'.

I mean, she convinced her daddy to give her the inheritance money *before* he died. She talked about making it while she was still young and then enjoying it when she was older, like *he* did, and he'd still be alive to see it and all and be proud as punch of her, and she came up with some fake business plan, and some fake products and an all-too-real lawyer she bribed to make her case for her, to sell Daddy on the whole nine yards, and when she promised to use her last name as part of the business name even if she got married later on, well, *that* was what sold the old geezer on the lot of it. I mean, daughters don't usually carry on the family name, now do they?

And here's one who said she would.

So he signed on the dotted line—the one that tears off real easy, the one that would separate him and her forever, the one that would connect the dots for Becca and me. I mean, she really knew how to play the old man and say the right things, just like I know how to say the right things to her. She came up with some real sweet phrases, like "following in his footsteps" and "continuing the Logan legacy" and "expanding Daddy's vision" into other areas she was expert in—all ones involving appearance, like makeup and fashion and design and all that, things he had no fucking clue about, things that he was sure as prayers on Sunday about that she *did* know. He knew she had the friends to make it happen too—I mean she ran in all those right circles, the ones with plastic smiles and silicone tits, so he knew that even with a little effort, she could make it fly. And this way, he'd even be around to see it happen and brag to his buddies about her.

What he didn't know is that she didn't want to work.

And the millions he gave her was more than enough for the two of us to start life together over here in *Pwairto Reeko*, which is kinda how they say it here, and it don't reek at all as it turns out, it's just a place where we didn't even have to change our passports to get to and live, a place he'd never think to look for his Hollywood-lovin' glitz and glam daughter of a girl.

I don't have to be the hard-ass jock all the time here either, and she doesn't have to dress to impress if she doesn't want to, though she likes to from time to time—I mean, there's no more livin' up to others' expectations, so we cut all ties, just like that umbilical snip the doctor gives. But these babies sailed far away from a family or two, not into one's waiting arms, and that's a giant difference—no cords or puppet strings that they can tug on anymore to reel us in with, play with us like some fish on a line, if you know what I mean.

So we're down here house huntin', well, condo-huntin' at the very least—like we need to make sure that the money lasts and all and we don't need some Princess Palace that will draw all too much attention or sprawl over acres we'd have to mow or pay someone to mow. We just wanted something that if we turn the key and step on a plane to some other exotic locale, that we won't have to worry a thing about—no plants that need to be watered or trimmed, pets that needed to be kennelled or pawed off on friends.

No cords. No strings. No ties at all.

And that's very freeing and I highly recommend it if you haven't tried it, but you know, it's got me worried too —more than a grow-op gangsta with a hydro guy and an IRS man knockin' at his door. *Whatcha usin' all that water for?* and all that, you know? Because, for me, it's riskier. At any time, she could walk away from this too—from me, even. And that would just kill me. And for me to start over? Now? Here? With no references or anything? I mean, I fucked off without saying shit to a soul, just like she did, so I imagine everyone back home's pissed at me or calling the hospitals or the morgue to check for a body. Like, I came here to be free and all, but it seems like Becca owns me now. She holds the dollars and seems to have all the sense.

But I've been spending some of my surfing time at the beach on the sand instead of on the water. Instead of riding the waves, I've been biding my time, thinking of the perfect way to put it to her.

And I came up with what I thought was a pretty good idea. I mean, I got some guy to wear a suit and follow us around, all suspicious-like. I told him which properties we were going to see and about when we'd be at each one, and all he had to do was show up wearin' that same suit each time—I mean, a full one with a vest and a jacket and tie and way too much for the weather, something she'd never miss—just smack her over the head with the thought that we was being followed like a Just Married car by tin cans. *That* kind of followed.

It was she who put the idea to me, which was just the way I wanted it:

"Do you think Daddy's tracked us here somehow?"

"Paper trail, I suppose," I said all calm and cool like. "With his connections, maybe even though we paid cash for the plane tickets—"

"He must have tracked us through the bank account. I wasn't sure he'd be able to free up that kind of information, but he must have used every cop connection he has to find us. I never thought he'd send the authorities after his one and only daughter or wish me any kind of harm. But the police must be involved, or else who is this mystery man stalking us?" She ran both hands through her long blonde hair, made fists of them once they were free again. "I can't go back now. I can't let him take me back. I'd be his prisoner forever if he got his money back, and he might write me out of his will for good, and—"

"So what do we do then?" I say all quiet-like, looking like she's the only one capable of getting a good thought.

"We need another city. We need our money out of that account. We need the safest safe we can find. I mean, there's no other way for us to stop looking over our shoulders, is there?"

I placed an arm around her shoulder and gently drew her in, reeled her in nice and slow, like a fish that's too heavy for the line, but a fish you aim to tire out and make yours all the same. That and a shoulder shrug was all it took from me. Less is more, remember? She taught me well.

So anyhow, we're looking for a place in another warm city right now, and that cash is safe in a safe and all, and she's not quite stupid enough to give me the combination or anything, and that safe's built into the wall and impossible to just cart away. So she's feeling quite sure of herself and all and we're looking for our new place, like I say.

She tells me she's more at peace now, and since we're not flaunting the wealth or anything at the moment, no one suspects that we have more than a fistful of funds between the two of us. We're no target, and there's no strange guy following us, and she's able to breathe now is what she tells me.

But the Prozac has returned, and I just pretend, real polite-like, that I don't see it.

She wants to be sure it's the place she wants, *the* place

she wants before she pulls out all the stops and offers them a cash deal for it. And she'll only make a deal with the owners themselves, no agents, just a friendly family that she knows will be moving far away to some other country like we did. No one left here to talk about the crazy Americans who pulled out a wad of cash to pay for the property. No stories about how much money we threw around. No loose ends. Just the couple we buy the place from and when they're gone, we're finally free for real, and that's that.

Well, the first place we see is just way too much, and I can see that right off: like a kitchen with some kind of marble backsplash and granite countertops and a bathroom with a bidet and imported Italian tiles, and built-in this, and custom that, and remote control something or other, and a steam shower and other un-necessities and of course, the crown jewels themselves—walk-in closets off the master bedroom that are big enough to live in.

And that's when I saw her give *that* look.

It was like she was time-machined back to endless shelves of shoes and closets of clothes and other girly graces—those riches she'd said she'd sacrificed for me. And there was that longing in her eyes—you know, like a rib-showin' bitch lookin' at a sirloin steak—*that* kind of hunger, and I knew right then that she was thinking of going back.

And after all I been through.

"Isn't it just *darling*? Isn't it *fabulous*? Don't you just *love* it?"

I mean, even her words were startin' to dress themselves up all nice and all and I could hear those old phrases comin' strong back at me like some billfold boomerang. "It's a beaut, dear, just like you. But—" I let my words trail off like that, like bait she'd be sure to take.

"But what?"

"But you don't want to settle on the very first one you see, do you? I mean, it's not like we can't rent for a while more and just take our time, check out a few others. Buyin' the first one you see would be like marrying the first boy you met in kindergarten without ever botherin' to check out the competition, you know?"

"Oh?" she says, and smiles like Miss Universe. "You mean like love at first sight? Like me and you?"

Shit. I mean, even when I don't want her to, she can push my buttons, and she knows it all too well, and I know if she pushed real hard I'd have agreed to it right there and then. But she surprised me when she said,

"Can't hurt to check out other options, do some shopping around, I guess."

And the way she said it and the look she gave me got me to wondering whether she meant she was getting back to her shopping addiction, or whether she was considering shopping around for a new boy toy too, and it got me thinking that I might just like to find out what that prissy Prozac was like for real first hand and by myself, you know?

And the next time I opened the medicine chest and saw that bottle there, and found myself craving what was inside like some nicotine addict who'd sell his grandma for his next pack of Marlboros if he had to—well, that's when I knew it had all gone too far. Me wasn't me anymore, and I wasn't even hittin' the weights hard like I used to, and some of those striations were startin' to smooth out, like pussy smooth, like Prozac smooth, no edge anymore at all, just a softness that made me sick to my stomach—same stomach the abs were abandoning one by one, and that freaked me out even more. Like why would she stay with me anymore if I let myself go too far?

So we're looking at this smaller place today—bachelor pad to end all bachelor pads—I mean, it doesn't even have an oven, just a hot plate, and it would hardly eat into any of the money at all since it's kind of one big room, no interior walls at all, just furniture strategically placed to create spaces—well, the kitchen counter kind of blocks the bed that's shoved off into a far corner, so it feels like there's a bit of privacy that way and all, but it's just the two of us anyway, right? So who cares?

But you step out onto this pathetic tiny thing they call a Juliet balcony, and what do you see? A sheet of blue, just wave after wave comin' in on you on a slow roll, but big enough to surf and all, and you know you can be on that beach in the time it takes you to take the elevator down from this fourteenth floor, and looking out over the rails here, it's like you're on a ship on the ocean anytime you want to be, and I realize I've found what I've always been looking for—that feeling of freedom I could have anytime I wanted it, anytime at all, and then I hear her say,

"Well, the view is pleasant, but this is *no* place for a couple. Shall we make an offer on the first one?"

So I hem and haw and act a bit baby-like and mope around not too much, just enough, just like she used to do when Daddy didn't let her buy the latest whatever, and she knows it's a real bug up my ass and I'm tryin' not to let it dampen her spirits and she doesn't know I'm trying to do just the opposite, so it shocks the shit out of her to see me this way, and it shocks the shit out of me and turns me transparent when she says,

"Well, I know how much you like it. What if we just buy both places and move back and forth between them?"

But even I know that's going to cost too much, going to eat into our living money. And I know she won't agree to buy just the place I want. So we're going to go back to look at the place one more time. The owner's got another offer in the meantime and he's going to sell it if we don't beat the price, so now, it's even more expensive. We've delayed on making a decision, so he's already shipped his belongings and is in a temporary stay situation at some hotel, ready to board a plane soon. I mean *that* kind of pressure.

But he's willing to give us another look. He'd love to see two people in love start their life together in a place that's meant the world to him. Romantic bullshit and all that, and here I was thinking guys just didn't buy into that crap for real and all. So anyway, he tells me "I can see how much you two are in love—wouldn't you love the perfect view to go with that wedding you're wanting?" And he hands me the keys and tells me to lock up when I'm done and all, and leave the key-ring with the girl at the front desk when I'm good and satisfied.

Well, I want to see the place by myself, just once. So I make some excuse and slip out, head over and up that elevator and out to the railing, that Juliet balcony, Mr. Romantic Pants, and I just lean out onto it like that *Titanic* broad and I can feel the freedom and I know what it's like at last, and I'm happy. I head back and tell the owner I love it and would love to bring a bottle of champagne and my wife to meet up with him again there that night. Tell him I think we'll have very good news for him and all.

So we return, the three of us, that night to see it, and I pretend real innocent-like to just think of the idea, tell Becca that the balcony makes it feel like we're on some cruise ship together, just like that chick in the flick with DiCaprio—and she gets that look in her eyes and squeals "*Titanic!*" and starts humming some Celine Dion song, rushing out to the balcony and leaning into that railing just like I did before.

Only this time, that railing gives, right in front of the owner and all.

I mean, he can see clearly that I didn't push her, wasn't anywhere near her, and somehow those screws that were never supposed to fail came clear out of smooth holes that looked like some carpenter ant or termite or somethin' had eaten around them for some time. And sure enough, they *did* find a few bugs that just could be to blame for it all, and how they got there, no one seems to know.

But I act all suicidal-like, like my life is over and how they're all to blame, and how my marriage is destroyed before it ever started, and the owner's worried about getting sued, and the property owner's worried about getting sued, and they offer me a pile of cash and a free place with the same view and a reinforced railing, and they fix all the others too and fumigate the place and now I've got it all—almost all the cash we started with, no one to have to split it with, no cords, no strings, just surf and the latest tits and teeth.

And I mean, I make like I have a few bucks to reel 'em in with, then after I land 'em and treat 'em like they're baitfish, small ones that need to be tossed back, they come at me even more. All tits and teeth, like I say, and one follows another like a silicone assembly line. Soft and silvery, like a school of mackerel—but I'm the one schoolin' them.

Each thinks she can be the one to change my playboy ways, to get me to settle down and all, to make her dreams come true, at least long enough for a divorce and a sizeable settlement. What they don't know is that I've played that game myself and I can see their moves from a mile or two away—or at least, from fourteen floors up.

You see, all I have in my bachelor pad is a bit of this and that, a big comfy bed, no medicine cabinet at all, and a fully stocked fridge and fully stocked gym. I mean a gym with all the bells and whistles, weights that make a *click-clack* backbeat track when I'm really hittin' 'em heavy. *Gold's Gym. Golden Gym.*

Gold-digger's Gym.

And I smile at that and wonder if Becca ever knew I only liked her for her...money.

MENOS COCA, MÁS CACAO

(Less Cocaine, More Cocoa)

The land is my love—a land of happiness and hopelessness, of beauty and brutality. And Chocó, Columbia is my home. It speaks to me in the evening, warm breezes breathing on my neck, soft wisps of wind winding their way around me in a late-night caress.

I'm awake and I'm outside for the same reason as always. I'm having trouble sleeping. And it's a good thing too, because the motorcycles? Well, I hear them long before I can see them, so I race inside to warn father.

Darse prisa!—Hurry up!—I whisper loudly in my father's ear, and I shake him awake. And I don't have to explain why. He helps me open the hatch on the floor, and together we gently lower it on top of us. It has the cheapest and ugliest rug we could find glued on top of it, so we're quite confident no one's going to want to steal it and discover our secret.

In minutes, we hear them tearing up our home, breaking everything that can be broken, knocking pictures off walls, smashing glass. I can hear objects falling to the floor, fracturing above our hiding spot. And I don't dare breathe. It's a tight space and I panic about making the slightest sound.

Chica tonta—silly girl—with all the noise they're making, they'll never hear us. But it's serious too, because if they ever discover us, they'll kill us both. Just like *mi madre*.

I don't know how long we wait before coming out, but I know it is hours, not minutes. Our house looks like a garbage dump inside, and we don't dare look outside. Not yet. Once I'm certain that my father is okay, I slip out the back, hop on my bicycle, and tear into town.

Because the land is my love, but Hector Trujillo is my lover. And he's a police officer too.

It's early morning when I reach his home and use the key he copied for me. I aimed to surprise him in bed, but as soon as I step inside, he is there, fully clothed, so I think I'm the one surprised.

"*Chica bonita,*" he starts to say, but stops just as quickly when he sees my eyes. "What's wrong?"

"Well, it's like this." I can feel the tears coming, but I fight them away. "It's easy for my father and me, but harder for you and me."

He pulls me close, wraps his arms around me.

I go up on tiptoes, whisper in his ear: "We move or we die."

And that sounds like an easy choice, but it isn't. Because Hector is here. And the land is here, and it's all we own. And Hector still lives with his parents too, and it wouldn't be fair asking him to take in two more. We move or we die. We move, and we're penniless and homeless.

Or we die.

The Black Scorpions are forcing farmers from their land. They give it up freely, escaping with their lives, or they sell it for a song. More fields for coca.

"You're safe with me. I'll look out for you," Hector says.

And I want to believe him. His name means "tenacious"—like a fighter—but I see worry in his eyes now too.

He pulls me up the stairs and to his bedroom and orders me to stay with him, at least until sunrise. And his offer is so tempting. His parents are in a bedroom down the hall. He's beside me. People are all around for my protection. In the end, the idea of a police officer in my bed is just too much to pass up and I tuck myself under the covers and pull them up to my chin. I'm not interested in sex tonight, and he knows it, so he just pulls me close. The warmth of the covers, the warmth of his body. I'm lulled like a baby in a cradle, and for the first time in weeks, I sleep.

And I dream pleasing collages and curious collections of images—warm places, smiling faces, my mother—but then the startling image of my father as a fountain of blood. I jerk awake, choke on my own saliva, and reach for

Hector, but he's nowhere to be seen. I know he worries about me. I know he's gone to check on Father.

I hear his motorcycle and rush to the window to see him tear off down the road. But I can't wait for him to tell me if my father's okay. I need to be there. I shouldn't have left him alone. So I dart downstairs, take the family car keys from a ceramic bowl near the entrance, and race outside.

I know what he'll say when I catch up with him. *Chica tonta—silly girl. Nothing to worry about, see?* But I can't help it, so I find myself with the pedal all the way down, rushing down a road at a speed I'm not sure I trust myself to drive. I'm expecting to fly off into a ditch at any second when, all of a sudden, I'm there.

I see Hector's motorbike outside, but I also see a black car I've never seen before. Did someone sneak up on him? Is he okay?

I park on the road and sneak to the window. When I look inside, I don't see Hector, but I see three other figures, all dressed in black, masks pulled over their faces. Black Scorpions. Two are on either side of my father, holding his arms. The third slips directly behind him and slits Father's throat in one swipe.

I'm frozen in place and see two images I'd never wished to see, ever. My murdered father, of course. And the man behind him who now removes his mask.

Hector.

"*Cerveza*?" he asks the other two, and when they nod and find a seat, he heads off in search of the beer.

I'm rooted to the ground even though I know it's simple.

Move or die.

So I will my feet to find their way back to the car. And I pull quietly away and pick up the pace once I think I'm at a safe distance to do so. I make one quick stop, and then head over to Hector's, returning the car to the exact space it was parked in out front earlier, returning the keys to the ceramic bowl, returning myself to his bed. And I pull up the covers to my chin and wait.

It's much later—hours, not minutes—when I hear him enter the room. He undresses fully—I can hear each piece as it falls to the floor. I'm up against the wall in a tight space where there is no escape.

But as he pulls back the covers to climb in next to me, the image I've created gives him quite a shock too.

I'm fully clothed. In fact, I wear extra shirts and pants of his over top of my own, and I have on a pair of rubber gloves that go all the way to my elbows.

In one hand I'm holding a golden poison dart frog, the one I've just stolen after breaking into the reserve we have right here in Chocó. Chocó, Colombia, a land of happiness and hopelessness, of beauty and brutality. My home.

The frog has enough poison in its skin to kill twenty humans on contact.

And I think of my mother. And I think of my father. And I think of one sweep of the arm.

And I rub that frog all over my lover's body, and run out the bedroom door and down the stairs. And I step outside and let the frog go, peel the gloves from me so they're inside out, and stuff them in the trash can.

And Hector is naked and he's not coming after me.

And Hector is naked and he's frozen in place.

And it's a simple decision, really—move or die.

And he doesn't move.

And it all makes sense. A Black Scorpion taken down by a golden frog. Darkness defeated by light. Bitterness by sweetness.

Menos coca, más cacao.

FLASHMOB FISHERWOMAN

Rebecca Denae grabbed her cell phone and texted:

> Times Sqr. Rockefeller Ctr. 7. Wear all black. W8 togthr. Brng othrz.

The location wasn't important. It's just that one of her favourite tailors, one near there, had finished with her new power suit and she couldn't wait to try it on.

The time wasn't important. She just wanted to get to the store before closing time.

And the colour wasn't important, either. It wasn't symbolic or anything—it was just that most people had black clothing, shirts and pants, so it was an easy uniform.

In the beginning, it was all about being able to pick

them out of a crowd. But now, after their group had grown, it was more about being able to see them *as* a crowd.

Be a fisher of men, the Bible said. And she was doing God's work. Under the guise of environmentalism, she'd netted herself quite a group so far. She didn't really care that much about the cause—well, of course she respected *all* of God's creations—but it was more of a means to an end. Once people were highly passionate about one thing, it was easier to get them to transfer that passion to something else.

And it *was* almost time to start bringing in the religious references. Not too heavy, no Bible bashing, just symbols to start with.

She'd be the Flashmob Fisherwoman.

Talk to people where they were first, and *then* convince them to go where you wanted them to go later. It was all for a good cause, whichever way you looked at it.

She slipped her feet into her favourite Lucci Delano alligator skin stilettos, the ones with the three-and-a-half-inch heels. Dreadful creatures, those gators, but they certainly made nice shoes. At least they had a use. All in God's plan, all in God's plan.

She picked up a package from the kitchen counter, a parcel she hadn't even dared to open yet after she'd raced it home from the shop. She upended her fox fur handbag, emptying the contents completely. Then she placed the parcel at the bottom, and carefully arranged everything on top of it again. There. If she ran into anyone she knew, and they happened to glance into her big shoulder bag, they wouldn't see any pink paper or red ribbon that they might just ask her embarrassing questions about.

She stepped to the closet, stilettos clacking on the bamboo floor like the tick tock of a clock, but stopped at the hallway mirror to take a peek at herself. Just a quick peek, she thought, not something vain. Just making sure that her temple looked taken care of.

She furrowed her brow at what she saw. Reaching long slender fingers inside her blouse, she fished out her cross pendant, allowing it to dangle freely outside, shining brightly against the dark blue silk. "Relationship with God," she said, drawing a long vertical line in the air. "Relationship with others," she said, crossing it.

She opened her closet and pushed her large chinchilla fur to the side. It wasn't quite cold enough for that yet, so she went with the mink instead. It had cost her an entire week's pay, but it was worth it. One touch and she was in heaven. She wouldn't do it up, though—it wasn't really that cold, after all. And that way, the cross would still show through.

She took the elevator down to parking level two, beeped her Mercedes SLK Showcar, and sank into the soft leather seat. She didn't really need to turn on the seat warmers, she knew, but it made the smell of the leather fill the air, a real smorgasbord for the senses, so she couldn't really resist. "Forgive me, Lord, for giving in to this one temptation," she said. "I am human, after all."

The radio was already tuned to her favourite station: FISH 105.1. The 5.1 made her think of Luke 5:10: Then Jesus said to Simon, "Don't be afraid; from now on you will fish for people." She preferred other translations. The ESV said, "from now on, you will be catching men." She took a quick peek at her long lithe legs and smiled. "I could, I really could if I wanted to, I think."

Then she laughed and said The New Living Translation aloud: "from now on, you'll be fishing for people." But her favourite was still the Aramaic Bible in Plain English: "you will be catching men for salvation." Well, women too of course. The Rebecca Denae version would read, "you will be saving people from themselves."

She'd use the valet parking at a nearby hotel—no use having to hunt around for a safe spot for her car, and it'd likely be impossible anywhere near Times Square anyway. Besides, the offering had been especially good at all of the services this week, and she *was* doing all this work outside the church too, with no one even knowing about it, except God of course, and she *was* his servant, so really, the money was being used to help Him in a way.

59th and Lexington, and one of her favourite shops—Bloomingdale's. When she reached the counter, she didn't dare open the bag containing the suit then and there. She had the receipt. If there was anything wrong, she could always return it. Besides, all the other times, things had been done to a T. She made the sign of a cross again. To a T. Smiling, she paid the bill and hustled out of the shop.

She headed over to Black Fox Coffee—another twenty-minute detour—but quality is worth the wait, after all. She could change in their washroom, then take time to relax on those soft comfy couches before heading over to see her godly soldiers. But it turns out someone was already using it, and they were taking their time about it too. Rebecca stood sipping her steaming hot cappuccino tapping her toe against the floor. *Love, joy, peace, PATIENCE* she reminded herself. Remember those fruits of the Spirit.

At last, the woman came out, and Rebecca slid in, bolting the lock, hanging her outfit on the door hook. She unzipped the bag, and had a pleasant surprise—she'd completely forgotten about the matching leather jacket she'd ordered with it at the time, but that was in there too. She'd keep her mink on though and try the jacket on later at home. But before she did any of that, she put paper towels all over the floor, stepped out of her shoes onto them, slid out of her slacks and dumped them in a heap (she'd have them dry cleaned later anyway), then dug into her purse for the package at the bottom.

She tugged the red ribbon, and let it fall from the parcel onto the floor. She tore at the paper, and then held out the fishnet stockings and let them dangle down from her hand. She was a fisher of men, after all, and she'd never be able to wear these to church, so this was her chance. Well, she wouldn't wear them *outside.* She'd put them on and slip her new pair of slacks overtop, so no one would see them, but *she* would know they were there, and that's what was important.

She rolled them down to the toes then slipped one foot, then the other inside. As she pulled the black strands slowly up her legs, she felt like she was officially part of the team. She wouldn't be with the others in front of Rockefeller of course—that just wouldn't be proper, and what if something happened, if police came?—but this bit of black identified her with them. She was their leader without a face, but she knew what *they* looked like when they were all together, and she wanted to feel more a part of that.

Her suit fit perfectly—that Antonio was a master craftsman with a pair of scissors and a needle, or whatever it was that he used. She loved the suit jacket too, but she wanted her mink, so she put the jacket back on its hanger, hung the pants from the floor on the hanger too (she would have to dry clean them *both* now), and used handfuls of more towels to gather up all the mess and stuff it into the wastebasket.

She was in a hurry now, though, to get to the spot to see them all assembled, and as she came out of the washroom, she had to push past *three* people who were blocking her way, just standing there by the washroom door. People could be so inconsiderate sometimes!

By the time she was a block away, she could see the throng before her—at least a few thousand strong—the street seemed fuller than ever. She found a safer spot about half a block away, and texted The Voice:

PETA POWER! PETA POWER! PETA POWER!

At first, she could only make out his strong voice, the one she called Simon, the one the others knew as The Voice. But within a few minutes, the place was rocking.

"Now hold up your hand," she said.

He did as he was told. The ones nearest him quieted down first, and they turned to calm those closest to them, and so on, and so on.

"New York is filled with materialistic muck!" she wrote. He shouted the words the next instant. While he did so, she continued to feed him lines: "Everyone is out for himself. It's become what can I buy, not what can I save. And no one seems interested in saving. Not in saving the animals, not in saving other humans."

The messages were being relayed through the crowd and there was an energy building. Rebecca slid one hand down to her pants leg. When she pressed hard, she could feel the outline of the fishnets.

Was it time? Was this the moment? It felt like it. She texted, "We must be a fisher of men!" How she longed to hear those words. It was the perfect time to hear them. And when she heard them from The Voice, the people responded. They were getting louder, cheering, and—

And he was still talking? She hadn't texted a thing. He was yelling something at them now, yelling and pointing. Pointing...down the street...at...her?

She saw thousands of heads turn in her direction. Then the crowd began to move as one. They stopped traffic and ran across, heading directly for her!

Rebecca dropped the clothing bag right there on the street, and did her best to run in her alligator stilettos. But she caught a heel in a sidewalk grating and a second later, she heard the sickly sound of it snapping from the sole. She quickly pulled off both shoes and raced away, but ten steps later, had to abandon her mink coat as well. The fur was just too hot and she was already almost out of breath.

She could hear the voices and the screaming, closer to

her now: “Murderer! You skin the animals—we skin you!” The first hand gripped her at the neck and pulled back.

And then there were more. And more after that.

She heard the tear of expensive silk, felt her power suit being pulled from her. And after her clothes were stripped from her body, and she was nearly naked as Eve herself, they left her wearing only two things as she lay there on the cold hard cement.

Her crucifix, of course, that chain around her neck that felt a bit tighter at the moment...the chain of an anchor.

And fishnets, with huge holes torn into them.

(DON'T) CONNECT THE DOTS

The first spot was the Vancouver Art Gallery.

Now I know what you're thinking—you? There? And I have an answer for that. You see, when you spend your days mucking stalls and stalling in muck; when you're smelling manure and you're smelling like manure; when you're carrying, constantly carrying—grain crumbles for the chicks, with the pink bucket, grain mash for the chickens, with the black bucket, hay for the cows, with the wheelbarrow, and meat and bone meal for the pigs, with the slop buckets; when you discover that the "solution" for too many feral cats on the farm involves rocks and a gunny sack, and twine, and a river, then you'll understand how I hungered for the highbrow, how I craved culture, how I made myself memorize Nehru's wise line: "Culture is the widening of the mind and of the spirit."

So that's how I came to be there when I first moved away from home, and found myself in the middle of an exhibit on loan from the Art Institute of Chicago: *Georges Seurat: (Don't) Connect the Dots.*

Apparently, Seurat invented pointillism, painting with little dots of colour that don't actually touch each other. Considering that some of his paintings were seven feet tall and ten feet long, it must've taken him more than a while to make those millions of spots.

But I couldn't stand and admire his works for long, mainly because I couldn't stand the spectators. One gentleman who looked like he was dressed for the opera approached me and said, "*Sunday Afternoon on the Island of La Grande Jatte* epitomizes the Neo-Impressionist method, but also the Post-Impressionist aesthetic." I know, right? And as I shifted over away from him, this librarian-looking lady, complete with one of those chains that hangs from the ends of eyeglasses, well, she nodded over to another painting, *Bathing Place*, and then she leaned in real close and whispered to me, like it was a secret or something, "There's a mysterious equilibrium between the eternal stasis of an Athenian frieze and the unceasing restlessness of a fugue." I forced myself to focus on the hard words anyway, but even when I searched them out later on, I still had no idea what she was going on about, and you know, I don't think she really did either.

You can see why I decided to leave the main exhibit and check out other parts of the gallery where there weren't so many weirdos around. And that's when it happened, and I didn't know why. I mean, Balthus' *Girl and Cat* stopped me dead in my tracks because, well, it just didn't look right—like something you could actually hang on your wall and have grandma see too—which was why it was in a museum, maybe. She's at an awkward age, a young girl entering puberty. And is she innocent or not—it's hard to say. She's got a bit of swagger, leaning back, arms behind the head, but all the light in the painting seems to be shining off the pale skin of her inner thighs. She's stretched out on a chaise lounge, and she's got a leg crooked up in front of her, and that's what makes the skirt slide back and show the bright white panties. Her socks are down around her ankles too, and she's not even paying attention to the cat or anything. Tabby's just there, on the floor beside her, the same as a shoe might be.

And I didn't want to look away, but I didn't want anyone to see me staring at this little Lolita either, thinking there might be a thing or two wrong with me. So I basically willed my legs around the corner, into another hallway, and that's where I saw the painting that put me under. I've learned since that it's one of Dwayne Harty's, a fairly realistic picture of a mother grizzly and her three young cubs. The mama bear has her paw resting on a giant rock, and there's a mountain poking its peak up through a cloud far behind them. It's called *Strength and Vulnerability*, and I'm not sure whether it was the title or what that got me, that made me faint, but you know, it's that age-old thing—people who build too close to the animals, and it's the animals, not the people, who are shot because of it. Well, the long and the short of it is that the gallery was the first.

The second spot was the Vancouver Aquarium.

Now don't get me wrong—I don't pick public places to pass out in so that I'll get some kind of sympathy from strangers. That's not why I was at the aquarium. I was there to see the sea otters. Sea otters are my favourite because they're smart and clean. They know how to use rocks like tools to crack open shells, and they take pride in keeping themselves perfectly spotless. I like clean, especially after the farm and all. Because otters have loose skin and an extremely flexible skeleton, they can reach any part of their body, clean themselves just like a cat. Better even. So it's no wonder with a flexible body like that and all that they can do those backwards somersaults in the tank so effortlessly.

This was my place of peace, my reward after the hospital stay, and if I'd just stayed at the tank or went back the way I came, I'd have been okay. But the smell of popcorn pulled me over like I was on a leash, and I ended up close to the polar bear enclosure. Back in the day before that poor bear died. So anyway, I looked over and saw that bear licking and licking a metal pole and then walking back and forth, pacing like a patient from *One Flew Over the Cuckoo's Nest*—you know, the dancing guy who never says a word in the whole movie?—and just like that, I dropped faster than a seagull spotting a sardine. Gave myself quite a bump on the skull there too.

And that's what's so strange about what happened next. I mean, it had been years and years with no spell at all, and then out of the blue it happened again.

The third spot was my family home.

Now, okay, I was dealing with the death of a parent, so that could be a part of it. When both Mom and Dad passed on, the farm, and its mountain of debt, was left to me. I'd have to sell it off to pay the bills, of course, but even then, there would be a little left over, so it wasn't like I was going to be bankrupted because of it. It wasn't finances that made me faint.

What I dreaded doing was packing up the house. I mean, I guess I could have left it for the new owners to deal with, but it wouldn't be fair to them, and I was certain it'd mean a lower selling price. My folks weren't millionaires, so I didn't expect to find anything valuable, but I thought I'd best look through to make sure something important didn't go to the dump.

I decided not to start with my old bedroom, but instead went about my work like any former farm girl would—methodically, meticulously, meaningfully. I didn't want to start with the creepy attic, so I decided to go the other way—down to the basement, and then work my way up.

As soon as I opened the door to the basement stairs, a scrawny farm cat sprang out—and even *that* didn't give me the scare it might have, and I'm thankful I didn't faint then and there and go for a two-second tumble down the stairs. When I did get to the bottom, there were already piles of boxes there waiting for me. It looked like my parents hadn't used the basement for years and had just turned it into storage. I'm sure Mom started all this as she felt her days coming to an end, but I stood there wishing she had thrown more out. Imported prairie people from Saskatchewan, hoarders at heart. But at least it was neat.

What wasn't so great was that it was the very first box I opened that floored me.

Staring up at me, soft, brown, arms open for a hug, was my very first teddy bear. Well, my only teddy bear—I've never had one before or since.

And just like that, it all came clear. And I worked it all out for myself. And I thanked my kind psychiatrist, I thanked you for your time and said I wouldn't be seeing you again. I marched out of that office knowing I'd never faint again. I knew it now. I knew what bit me.

The bears. The bear. The teddy bear I had spent so many nights staring at—the one with no sharp claws and no sharp teeth, no way to protect itself or me. The one whose eyes I'd stared into helplessly as a child whenever I felt Daddy's hands on me from behind.

No, Seurat's got it all wrong, I decide. Sometimes you have to connect the dots in order to see what's past them.

SEVEN SHADOWS

A shadow is you and not you, at the same time—a distortion, an illusion, a fun-house mirror image that is everything, that is nothing. It lives in the future or lags in the past. It leaps to locations you've not yet been to, it lingers at sights you've already seen.

It is with you and not with you, and the closest you ever get is when, directly overhead, a bright sun puddles one at your feet. It stubbornly stays with you, a piece of gum on the sole of your shoe, one that's lost its flavour, one that's lost its stretch.

It disappears only in darkness, hiding there, lurking in the black of night, hoping for some headlight to spring it back to life.

Those are your shadows.

But the shadows of *my* family stay with me.

"Empty the bag," the one beside me says, so I turn it over, end for end, shaking out the contents. Seven rough wooden circles of different sizes with symbols carved into them tumble out:

A rope.
Stars.
Barbed wire.
A bee.
A hand.
A hammer.
A lock.

And he asks me what they're for, and I ask him how much time he has. I mean, how do I explain that these are the shadows of my family? And the bag I keep them in is old and worn with a drawstring that's fraying, and he says that there's no way he can let me keep them in something so old and tattered like that, so he takes the bag away and I really wish he wouldn't have done that.

Because the pieces are my friends, enemies, and relatives.

But the bag is me.

And he returns with a cardboard box for me to put them in, but I leave them out to help me tell my story.

I pick up the first of my personal runes, the rope.

It's easy to explain, and it's hard to explain, and that's the way it is with a shadow, I suppose.

My father was born in Weldon, Saskatchewan, in

drought and poverty. He'd lived through tornados blowing topsoil clear to North Dakota, heat waves toasting crops to crumbs. It hardened him, toughened him, twisted his body into ropes of muscle accustomed to plowing through heavy labour as long as there was daylight.

By the time he was 37, he had a farm, a wife, an unmanageable mortgage, and twin 12-year old daughters his wife was doing everything in her power to keep from becoming tomboys.

But there are no lives of leisure, no glittering tiaras, no beauty pageants on the prairies—just lines and lines of barbed wire staked to fence posts that keep you in and others out, and you learn soon enough that it's not easy and it's not pretty, and those barbs aren't built to lean on.

So one day during calving season, my sister, Kaitlyn was with him as he visited a heifer in trouble. And I can tell you that story, but I need to change some of the details so the dagger doesn't slide in too deeply:

BIG RED SCHOOLHOUSE

I was fresh from university,
and my uncle said I had to listen
to the land to get what it would teach me,
that the barn was a big red schoolhouse if I was
a willing student, and what I didn't get then,

I remember now,
the slaughter in winter, back when zero and below
made sure carcasses would not rot,

how we herded cattle single file
like school kids to assembly,
back when zero and below made metal runs bone cold, and

I remember
making my way in winter, in zero and below,
to the front of that line, with my uncle, Sid,
him smashing that hammer hard between the eyes,
when zero and below could anesthetize, and

I remember
lifting the back legs high in winter,
back in zero and below, before plunging,
bone deep, too deep, just above breastbone,
cutting high above backbone,
and severing arteries, bleeding her out,
when zero and below made all that blood run too, too slow

Now I'm back
crouching in the springtime,
squatting on one stump and eyeing another–
third knuckle of my uncle Sid's left hand–
knowing there's no further growth for either one,

and I'm sitting there, doing my best James Dean,
cigarette hanging from the corner of my mouth
like an afterthought, like an ivy that snakes
its way down to long slender fingers, *whole*
fingers, contemplating its next move

And it's springtime, and it's calving season,
and at first I think *birth and beauty, new life,*
like clean clothes fresh off the line, like fresh
cream into butter, just better and better,
but then we hear the moan, a low groan
from the ground, and the heifer's on her side,
and I jump off that stump, stomp the cigarette
and my work boot into muck,

ankle deep

She's not asleep and dreamin', that's for sure,
is all I hear my uncle say, and he looks at my
monogrammed sweater and he looks at my
crisp new blue jeans, and he just shakes
his head, like *I'm* the one in trouble,

And I'm standing there, me, the one with the skinniest arms,
and he brings the loop of rope from the barn, and he asks me
if I know what it's for, then waits no more, just points
to the heifer and says, *Calf's stuck. You're going in,*
boy—into the pelvis, he means,

elbow deep

to hook the leg back into line, then push
forward, down, then back, and pull
like hell, and it's anything but pretty
and there's too much blood
and I'm flat on my ass, new jeans

covered in manure, sweater
coated with slime, hands
raw from the rope,

and it's then I'm being schooled,
and start thinking
about that finger,
about the baler twine tugged tight around, pulled clear
through,
about how beauty can be ugly,
like my own fine mess,
like how that stump of a finger
shows a hand that knows hard work,
like that calf, standing tall right now,

sucking on the udder of a dead mother.

A rope and a mother and a calf. A rope and a father and a child. And that child was 12, not 22, and a girl, not a young man, and she never did smoke or own nice clothes or make it to university, and that makes it all the more tragic somehow.

Kaitlyn never did quite get over it. For the rest of the day she stared at that dirty, slimy blood-drenched rope, turned it over and over, like a guilty kid wringing her hands, and we thought we knew why and we gave her space. And she went to bed early, and she got up early, and by the time the rooster crowed, we saw her swinging from that rope, her body a pendulum suspended by the barn loft above.

And her body kept moving, but time didn't for me.

Strong rope.

It didn't break.

And because I was the first one out the door that morning, I was the one who lowered her, loosened that rope, and removed it from her neck.

And I curled into the dead body like I was a foetus and stayed there until Mama came and collapsed on top, hugging both bodies, a live one and a dead one, and we stayed like that a great while, I suppose. I swore I could hear a baby's heartbeat inside Kaitlyn even then, but Mama said "Stuff and nonsense" and wasn't willing to talk much after that.

It was Aunt Sarah who saved me. She taught me about poetry, made me memorize some lines from Robert Frost:

"When at times the mob is swayed
To carry praise or blame too far,
We may take something like a star
To stay our minds on . . .

Poetry, and Aunt Sarah, became my stars, my way of making sense of nonsense. She showed me poetry in the Bible too, even some passages about ropes—how a cord of three strands cannot be broken, how it's stronger together than any strand is on its own. But I know that's not true, because Papa threw himself into work, and Mama became barbed wire or a mouse, depending on your point of view, so I had to be tough for the others.

Once I doubted the poetry in the Bible, I doubted the rest of it too, and I suppose it all started there for me.

The bee, all yellow and black? There was this Chinese family the locals allowed to stay in town since they opened a restaurant that catered to Canadian flavours. But then the black family moved in, and I expected them to be run out on a rail, but it got complicated when their son started dating the Chinese couple's daughter. Acceptable and not, you know? Black and yellow, a bee, and it created quite a buzz, even more of a noise than my sister's suicide, and I resented it and I hated how the Chinese girl had a boyfriend before I did, and that's when I left for good.

The hand is my first true friend, Lizzie. She extended a hand to me when I needed it, but she's not the hand because of kindness or strength or warmth, even though she took me in when others wouldn't. She's the hand because of skill—five-fingered discounts at Woolworth's and the like, enough to keep herself living a life away from home. And she taught me her skill and her attitude is my attitude, you know?

Get them before they get you.

And the hammer? That's someone who got me. Let's just say that the head of a hammer has two parts—one pounds and one pulls apart, and that's about all I can say about that at the moment.

The lock is obvious. It's the lock on my prison cell. It's the lock on my choices. Like the *real* reason you took my drawstring bag away, warden. I know what a bag and a rope can do. But remember, I'm the strong one, the one who carries it all with her, the one who holds it all together.

The failure of my parents.

The suicide of my sister.

The tragedy I've made of my own life.

I guess that sometimes, to move on, a cord *has* to be cut.

And he leaves and I wonder how much of my story he believes. Because when you slide from one foster family to another, you don't have any relatives and you make them up from scraps, from shadows of others to help people understand. Nothing too perfect—your mind won't accept it. So you slowly let other lives slip into yours and they walk with you throughout your days, and one morning you wake up and realize you don't remember what's real and what's a shadow, and you realize you no longer care.

And as I well know—you don't need a bag or a box to carry shadows with you.

And it's then that I realize that without the bag, there's no me. I think of a symbol I might make for myself.

I have no personal rune.

And I smile at the irony, even as I realize the hard truth:

Those seven shadows can be swallowed in one great gulp.

CHAMELEON

Grad 2021 is days away, and our high school is abuzz with talk of parties, prom dresses, and princesses—and a special little something called STING.

It's basically tag for teens. Every senior who offers up a ten-dollar ante gets the name of a victim-to-be, someone to stalk and tag outside of class time. You have to get a video of it happening, post it online, and if it's legit, you get the name your target had, and off you go, like some psycho *Survivor* contestant. Get that next name and kick them off the island that is Dr. Charles Best Secondary.

Last person standing gets $1600.

I'm certain serial killers are made this way.

I'm participating because everyone is participating, and because sixteen hundred is nothing to sneeze at, and mainly because it will help me pursue my next steps and escape this dead-end city and its tight network of Karens.

Middle-aged moms talking to middle-aged moms about their precious children.

Okay, if I'm honest, the money is the only reason I'm in it to win it. And if I'm honest, the real reason I've made it this far is all too clear—you think I'm invisible and you're right.

To you, I'm a chameleon that blends into any background. So far, you've spent more time avoiding your stalker than you have pursuing me.

And if I'm honest? I wish you'd chase me a little more.

And chameleons? My biology text says it's a myth that they melt into their surroundings.

It's more emotion than fight, more communication than flight. And my face is as open as a homeless person's hands and heart. So I could be an easy target.

But you think I'm invisible and you're right.

Three remain:

The Prom King. Antonio. You.
The Prom Queen. Ava. Her.
And the wallflower. Eleanor. Me.

And you have me.
And I have Ava.
And Ava must have you.

Hasn't she always?

There is no way she's about to end your game, so I know this is it. You're coming for me.

And I don't know whether to be scared or excited.

Scarcited, maybe.

And I can feel my face flush, that rising red tide that swims over my skin whenever I think of you.

I'm the Chameleon.

Picture it—one tag away from a face-to-face with you. One tag, and we're officially searching for each other. It's so Romeo and Juliet, and I can picture it perfectly:

We agree to split the prize money, and we find a very public place, like the courtyard out front of the school, the one where you meet daily with the other lacrosse jocks, and you strike that pose—one hand leaning on the back of the bench, while standing as far as you can from the garbage can on the other side of you.

No one would pick that spot to stand, no one, but you do it daily—it lets you flex your bicep while gripping the bench like a castaway does a life ring. I have the look engraved in my brain, but as I appear, you'll leave that bench and you'll leave those Cro-Magnon mouth breathers and you'll leave me breathless as we both reach our right hands skyward—we'll save the left hands for marriage—and we'll do a high-five in slow-mo, and friends will video the moment for posterity, and that's when I'll melt my fingers into yours and hold that hand just long enough for you to feel the heat rush from my face to my fingers and—

And she's there.

Ava. My target.

She's near the open area near the cafeteria, a small

lobby filled with tall radiators, where the Heater Kings and Queens of our school congregate to intimidate others outside of that group.

But she's surrounded by her entourage. Other Barbies with names that rhyme—Brandy, and Candy, and Sandy—and other things you call your children if you want them to grow up to be porn stars.

No wonder she's lasted this long. If anyone comes near, she has a football team of females blocking the way—if football teams wore pink, and lip gloss, and pink lip gloss, that is.

Chameleons have to sneak up on their prey. Even so, they're a bit geeky like me, and have a jerky walk—that maybe helps them blend in with rustling leaves and swaying branches—but my penguin walk definitely doesn't help me blend in. It's when I'm still that I'm unnoticeable.

That's when people like you think I'm invisible, and you're right.

I can't outmaneuver the entire Barbie brigade, so I need to outsmart them. It's the only way. If I try to break through that front line, they'll likely delay me and distract me, and you'll sting me from behind. Then King and Queen will split the prize money and I'll be left with a sting as a reminder of my stupidity. Left out in the cold, by the Heater King and Queen.

Left out in the cold . . . and that's when it hits me. I have a plan to knock out the dame with the palindromic name.

Ava, I'm coming for you.

Chameleons rely on stickiness to hunt. Each foot has two pads that squeeze together like a vice. The tail can wrap around tree branches. The tongue can shoot out more than twice its body length. And the spit is four hundred times more viscous than human saliva. Grippiness and stickiness—the Brandy's and Candy's and Sandy's would know all about that. Thank you biology textbook. Just like that, my plan is complete.

I just need to execute.

Chameleons can look in two directions at once. I can't. But as I creep down the hallway, my head's on a swivel. I can't let myself be taken by surprise, not when I'm this close.

Moments later, I'm flat on my back on a cold, hard surface. My eyes are focused on a narrow space. They're almost watering because I'm worried about blinking and missing my moment. I realize that where I am, if I move at all, if any movement is detected, I could be making myself an easy target. I'd never see it coming.

But this is worth it. My one shot.

I'm cramped, I'm uncomfortable, but my eyes are laser-focused on that narrow bit of daylight. Chameleons can zoom in on their prey like a telephoto lens, and I'm attempting to do just that. But I don't dare blink. I picture what you would see if you were looking for me.

And I think I'm invisible to you. And invisible to Ava. And I'm okay with that at the mom—

And just then, I see what I'm after—two Ava ankles. My tongue-hand shoots out to grab the right one as I slide out from under her car in the student parking lot. The other hand tilts upward and I catch her shell-shocked pretty in pink face—a look I want to make a giant poster of to remember her by. No need. I immediately post the video into the group chat and Ava is done.

Ding dong, the Queen is dead. Queen Bee? I don't think so. No more stinging for her.

The back of my shirt is destroyed from sliding across parking lot pavement underneath her car, but no Barbie could save her this way. Focus on the ankles near the driver's door. And it worked like a charm, and I race to my bicycle, leaning against a nearby tree, booking it away from the Barbie-arians before they recover from the shock and do me some damage.

I make a clean escape, Ava's words growing fainter and fainter behind me:

"FUCK! You're a fucking lunatic! You cheap little bitch . . . "

And I'm gone.

It's down to the two of us. The King and the Chameleon. King's Chameleon?

Chameleon's King? I'd be okay with either, frankly.

And I know Ava will tell you the whole sordid tale of how she got stung by a mouse. I mean, the video is there for all to see. Even those who thought they knew what I was like before will see me in a whole new light. My true colours are on display for all to see. The ones that show how conniving I can be.

That bright red pigment painting me as a target.

You'll be extra vigilant now, and you'll get the entire school to spy on me, report on my whereabouts at all times. Can't have a wallflower winner, right?

So I need to cut my losses. Act fast, before you think it through.

I compose the e-mail carefully, showing the King why he should make me his new Queen, at least to split the prize money. Neither of us will walk away empty-handed. I make my best case, telling him that just like Ava never saw me coming, he won't either, so would he like to make a quick $800 or would he like to make MAYBE nothing?

I send it and wait for the rejection. Hell, he'll know he has the backing of the entire student population, and I've got mainly myself. He has every advantage. If I were him, I'd be one hundred percent confident of a win, and I'd want that $1600 to myself, all to myself, or even $800 to splurge on Ava to make myself a hero to her all over again.

So imagine my surprise when he says . . . "Yes."

The plan is to meet in the courtyard before school the next day. Plenty of witnesses.

We'll walk towards each other with our right hands high. As we approach, we're supposed to say, "We both tag at the same time. STING has TWO winners this year."

Epic moment. It'll be like *Hunger Games* and the poison berries. *Survivor* with two winners? Mind-blowing. And people will snap endless photos of it happening. And those photos will circulate, percolate through social media. And Ava will see my hand touching Antonio's and her colour will rise.

All the photos of me and Antonio. And Ava—invisible, with the colour change? She'll be the new chameleon, and maybe, just maybe, I'll convince Antonio to make his co-winner his new Queen, his prom date. After all, who wants to go with some crazed female control freak, right? Which is what I can count on Ava morphing into at that moment.

Yes, it was all coming together. Everything in place, everything perfect.

So when the morning arrives, and I don't, he's pissed. He gets louder and louder: "SHE is pushing for a deal and now she's screwing me over? FIND HER! Find that little whore who took out Ava!"

And those words sting me like nothing else could. And as you strike a pose, that pose, one hand gripping the bench hard, the other waving wildly in the air, I can feel the blind rage.

I'm invisible to you. In all ways.

So as your left hand points towards the school, it passes over the garbage can, and my left hand shoots up like a sticky tongue, gripping you by the wrist, and my right hand takes the video.

It's over.

I climb out of the garbage can, shake off the stench, and let you go. One quick video post, and it's over.

In all ways.

And you thought you knew my colours. And you thought you'd see me coming from way off. But the Chameleon? Screw the biology textbook—she can blend into her surroundings when the time is right.

And she can ignore her emotions and ignore clear communication and still have telephoto focus—eyes on the prize.

It's like I told you—I really need the money.

All $1600.
Flush beats straight.
Chameleon takes the Queen.
Chameleon takes the King.
Checkmate.

CLUE

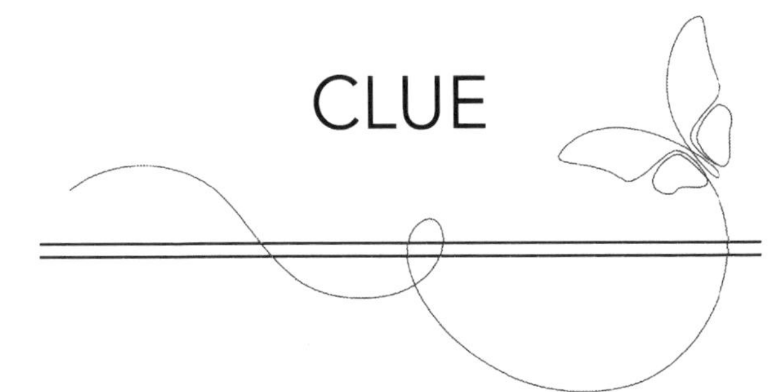

It was just another shitty Monday, but before the end of first block, we had a mystery on our hands—someone had stolen Principal McClosky's pipe. This was a crime of the first degree—I mean, you never saw the guy without it. Actually, he's the only person I've ever seen *with* one—but at school, he was cool with it. He never smoked in front of students, but he didn't hide out in the bathroom or head out to his car in the parking lot to sneak a puff either. He kept it out in plain view on his desk and used it kind of like a paperweight. You always saw him with it, touching it, holding it, cleaning it—just never smoking it—except outside of school of course.

Then, if anyone ever happened to run into the guy, they'd see that pipe dangling out of the corner of his mouth, creeping down out of it like an ivy, all natural-like, like it belonged there, like it'd always been there. Sometimes, it was lit, but never indoors. The guy was a considerate addict, and the students adored him for it. Just rebellious enough to openly be a smoker, but nice enough not to make you inhale the crap yourself.

The biggest mystery was, first of all, how someone got it. I mean, when he was in his office, it was right there, usually in his hands. When he was out of his office, the door was locked. Whoever pulled it off had balls of steel, but he'd need 'em because he wouldn't exactly be Mr. Popularity around the school once he was found out.

Everyone was talking about it, texting about it, snapchatting and yapping in the hallways and cafeteria about it, and every classroom was full of whispers, but no one knew a damn thing. No one was claiming responsibility, and whoever had taken it was being deathly quiet about it. It was so weird—I mean, when it came to grad pranks, we always knew who was responsible, and most of them were listed openly on our fanpage on Facebook. But here was an inside job that nobody knew anything about.

I mean, I didn't know, and my boyfriend Jordan didn't know, and we're the kind of people that other people tell things to, you know? So we were kind of weirded out about it and all, but as it turns out, we didn't have to wait long for that mystery to be solved. By the end of the day, as McClosky turned from looking out the window and happened to glance at his desk, there was the pipe, sitting in its usual place, like it had never left.

I mean, freaky weird. So the stolen item was recovered, the lost was found, but we still didn't know who the thief was . . . until about a week and a half later.

Word is, it was the English teacher, Mr. Makarenko, who was the thief. McClosky found out at his retirement party.

The teachers knew he was trying to kick the habit, but they also saw how much of a habit he'd developed holding it, playing with it, cleaning it, so they knew he'd never let it go easily. They'd lifted it early in the day, taken it and made a cast of it, and then cleaned it and replaced it by the end of the day, teachers flooding McClosky's office and providing a distraction for both sleight of hand routines.

And at the retirement party, they presented him with an identical metal one that he could use like a paperweight if he ever, uh, decided to get rid of the real one for good, if you know what I mean. It was like a less than subtle hint for him to give up the habit. And engraved on the stem of it: "*You're a smokin' principal, with or without the pipe*"—or something cheesy like that, I heard. But it was another bit of news that caught my attention...news of what he planned to do next. Apparently, his first training was as a librarian and he'd already lined up a part-time position at the University of British Columbia, his alma mater.

Jordan wanted both of us to approach him at once, but I told him to lay low on that idea. I'd go to him first. He wouldn't be so suspicious that way. But I think I nearly gave the old guy a heart attack when I asked him, quietly, secretly one day, "Do you think you could pull a few strings over there somehow and let me get a library card at the university a bit early? I mean, I've been conditionally accepted anyway, and I'd love to be able to use their materials for my final history paper."

We had about a month and a bit left to the semester—our final semester, his final semester. But we really wanted the library cards for another reason. Okay, we were both good students who took care of our grades, and that's why we were already accepted into the computer science program at UBC, but we were pathetic in other ways. I mean our parents kept us both crazy busy and gave us zero privacy, so, just so you know, we wanted the cards because, well, we wanted a place where we could kind of make out and not be disturbed. Not make out, make out, but you know, the upper floors were usually kind of deserted, and if you picked the stacks at the back and weren't loud about it, you could get away with quite a bit.

For me, it accomplished two things. One, it gave my boyfriend a bit of fun—hands under my shirt or firmly on my ass, my long fingers dipping inside his pants, rubbing, rubbing—that kind of thing. A few touches, a few pinches, nothing stronger, nothing more. So he got a bit, but it wasn't like we were going to have an accident of any kind that would radically change our future. We were both too smart to let something get out of control, so the library seemed the perfect solution. I mean, neither one of us was about to drop our pants in a public place anytime soon.

I guess we COULD have gone to the library without a card, but our parents would never buy that. We'd have to produce some kind of books to show we were studying or researching there, and I don't think either set of parents would ever suspect what their honour students were really up to in the game theory and political science section of the fifth floor of that building. I had gotten a card, and of course, Jordan, being the A student he was, wanted to make use of it too.

That was what we told the adults.

They still insisted on dropping us off and picking us up. Remember—they had a lot invested in us, too, and so far, we'd been kept "safe" by them—no drugs and no sex that they knew of. We'd cart out some books that did or did not have anything to do with what we were studying at the time, and they beamed with pride, thinking we were just overachievers who were getting ahead of the rest of the pack. More scholarship money, that kind of thing.

Oh, and the second thing, one I didn't tell Jordan, was that I actually went there by myself sometimes too, to actually, uh, do research for my paper. No use wasting the card, right?

It was on one of my lone trips that I saw the guy for the first time. McClosky was there too, on a Saturday, getting some training and helping to check out books. The other guy was taking out a few heavy tomes, photo books filled with innovative architecture, but he seemed to be chatting with Mr. McClosky like they were old buddies or something.

College friends? Co-workers from another time? I didn't know and didn't really care. All I knew was that McClosky had style but this guy dressed weird. I mean, the first day I saw him he looked like a leprechaun—like Barry Weiss on that episode of *Storage Wars*, you know? Only I like Barry a lot more than I liked the looks of this guy. This forty-maybe-fifty-something man seemed like he was bathing in green—a real toxic fashion disaster.

McClosky didn't seem to say much—he just nodded and said a few "ahhs" and "I sees," all the while fiddling with the fake pipe in front of him. Maybe it was his Linus comfort blanket when dealing with *those* kinds of patrons. In any case, it seemed that, with the pipe in front of him, McClosky could be nice to anyone. I wondered how he'd act without it.

Well, I wondered for all of a few minutes. I mean, I didn't really think much about it, not then, and especially not during my next trip to the library, because, well, Jordan was with me, and we'd stepped up our game playing a bit. He was trying to rub and touch me anywhere but *there*, you know, trying to get me to let out a gasp or a groan that was loud enough that we'd have to stop for fear of being discovered. My goal was to rub and rub and clutch and grab and attempt to make him run for the nearest bathroom to avoid an embarrassing accident before *that* happened. I could tell he was doing his best to hold back, but I knew I was winning too, at the same time, and then he tweaked a nipple after not touching me there at all and he kind of caught me by surprise and I let out a loud "Ohhhh" just as I looked up into the eyes of *that* guy at the end of the stack, the guy who'd been talking McClosky's ear off that one time, the guy who had silently crept up on us and seemed to be watching, the perv.

He had on a dark green tie this time and a lime green fedora and when he saw that I saw him, he just made a *tch-tch* sound, shook his head, and walked away. Would he say anything about us to McClosky? I mean, I don't think Jordan cared if he did or not, but it mattered to me. No use destroying the old man's halo image of me for nothing.

Jordan headed for the nearest bathroom, and I decided to follow Lime Hat down to the checkout counter and spy on him just a bit, to see if he might report me. I don't know the reason why what happened next happened. Maybe it was the fact that he saw the two of us getting some and he hadn't lately—well, at least that's the reason I came up with later, after the arrest.

In any case, at the checkout, he was raising his voice and getting louder and louder. I half expected he was yelling at McClosky to do something about the two teens having sex in the book stacks, but that wasn't it at all. As I got a bit closer, he was outright shouting, and I heard,

"Is that it, then? You've got your fucking award and your fucking university position, and now you're too good for me? Or is it that you're ashamed to be seen with me with this stuck-up crowd? I embarrass you, do I?" He had both his hands on the counter and he looked like he might reach over and strangle McClosky in an instant.

"It's Jenkins, isn't it? Your new boss. You're fucking your new boss and you thought I'd never find out? Now you don't even want to be seen with me in fucking public?"

McClosky was looking down at his shoes like they were a work of art or something, but then he took these quick mouse peeks to see if anyone might be around to hear, and that's when he saw that I saw him. He was in shock and he still wasn't saying a word, and that wasn't helping the situation any. He reached for the paperweight and slowly tapped the pipe on the counter like he was emptying fake tobacco out of it or something. "You might want to—"

"You and that FUCKING PIPE!" Mr. Green Tie screamed, yanking the object from his hands. "Do you know what I think of your fucking pipe?" And just like that, his arm—so long, how had I not noticed it was so long before?—thrust out from his body in one quick jab, and the stem of the pipe embedded itself through the eye of old Mr. McClosky. It must have hit something delicate because the old man's body dropped to the floor like kids on Christmas morning, and Mr. Tie and all jumped over the counter and cradled him in his arms.

"I'm sorry. I didn't mean to. I mean—"

And he laid the limp body on the ground and grabbed onto the nearest chair and kind of tugged himself into it. I took out my cell, called 9-1-1, and in no time at all, campus cops were on the scene. He looked up to see me watching him this time, and he just stayed there as they cuffed him and turned to me, and Jordan, who was with me by this time.

And the officer closest to me asked if I was a witness and when I nodded yes, he whispered, "Just tell me what you saw."

I looked over at the dead old man and his murderer and I—I couldn't stop myself, I just started to fucking laugh. "It was—it was—"

"Just tell me," the officer said. "It's okay."

"It was Mr. Green, in the library, with a lead pipe."

NARROW ESCAPE

A normal day for me starts out that way, you know, normal, with all the usual stuff *you* do, like what you do when you rise up to the sunshine, right, but it almost always morphs into something other than that for *me*—like today, I'm headed to the zoo, going to race right for the elephants—those huge, lumbering grey beasts who are in no hurry whatsoever, like pensioners on park benches, and who need a lot of what I crave too, room—but I forget that to get to them, I need to pass the building that holds the snakes—including the boa constrictors, and one of their keepers is outside, sneaking a cigarette—how that smoke fills the air and must fill the lungs, choke out the oxygen, fill fresh spaces, fresh places, with bits of tar, making breathing just a little harder to do the next time, a little bit harder—and anyway, he was chatting to a buddy about something he'd heard about boa constrictors—and think about that name for a second, because we use boa to mean like a snake of feathers a woman might willingly wrap around her neck, and constrictor, well that's something that tightens, isn't it, like a necktie—yep, never wearing one of those never *ever*—and the keeper was explaining why boas don't suffocate themselves when they swallow prey whole—you can picture it, right, some rodent pressed up against both sides of a snake's throat, if they have throats, that is, so *how?*—and it turns out they can use different sections of their ribcage to breathe depending where the prey is—just swallowed, part way down, or being digested—and that breathing from the ribs makes me think of human ribs and how they cover lungs and how those lungs might have bits of sticky tar in them and be carrying out a slow suffocation that lasts years and years, and the problem is that humans can't breathe from their ribs now, *can we?*

Whew, so I hurry past the snakes and the guys and the snake guys who might really be guys who are snakes but I don't know them personally so who's to say—and the elephants may have a lot of room to roam, but there's a crowd outside that fence that surrounds the lot of them—hundreds(?) of bodies—seems like—and it seems those rib cages are all kinda mooshed up against one another, ribs like parentheses (   ) that keep words separated from other words, those ribs keeping the hearts apart so the beats don't boom together, combine in chaos, and everyone moves a bit this way and a bit that way, especially those in back, trying to get a better look at what would never fit in their own backyards—and I notice the red tie of the businessman and the orange scarf of the woman next to him, and the lanyard of keys dangling down from some teacher type—*Riverview Elementary* crawling down the strand around her neck—and a pile of kids surrounding her, giving her no space at all, some tugging at her clothing even, fingers curling closed over the cloth—and that pull and tug, like the too-tight leather belt around the Dad bod nearby, the one with the middle age spread, trying to suck it all in with leather cinched tightly around his waist, all pinched by a strap pulled one or two holes tighter than is comfortable, I'm guessing, and that makes me think of corsets and if women still wear those and if they do, well then, who laces them up so tightly for them, crushing their rib cages, pulling torsos in so tightly—and if not, well who was the first female who realized how this was never a good idea, never *ever*, and I think of other body parts crammed into tight spots, like toes into stilettos, legs into narrow fit jeans, and of course the ties and scarves and what possesses people to put nooses around their own necks freely—and to spend good money on something *like that?*

So the snake thing is too much, and the crowd's too big, and I'm smart enough to avoid the obvious, anything that looks like a cave or a tunnel or a tight space where people push in and have trouble turning around—and nothing with an elevator either, and not too many flights of stairs because really there's not much room between the handrail and the wall, and if I make one slip I might smack into one or the other, or one then the other, and then down the stairs, and if it's like the twenty-fourth floor or something, well who would look for me there, right, and the idea of having something on two sides of me is only slightly less terrifying than the idea of being surrounded by four windowless walls in a tiny box that moves at speeds it shouldn't be able to, and at that point what I'm really wondering is why elevators exist at all, and as I pass by the auto body shop, I see the mechanic right under the car that's jacked up overhead and I picture the teacher telling us to hide under our desks during earthquake drills and I don't feel safe at all, I just think that when the ceiling collapses and it pins us between our desks and the floor like jelly sandwiches, it just makes it easier and neater for the forklifts to come in later and lift us out in nice neat slabs—no fuss, no muss, nothing ugly for anyone to see as they clear us outta there, just nice, neat school sandwiches to be dropped into nice, neat rectangular holes somewhere made for such a disaster—graves the size of desktops.

And *that* image is not helping, and I can feel my heart, and at first it pounds slow and hard, with pauses in between: *BA!.....DUM!........BA! DUM!,* but then it lightens and quickens, like the music's picking up: *ba!dum!ba! dum!ba!dum!* and three beats take the time of two before, and my steps quicken and my pulse does too: *bdum! bdum!bdum!bdum!,* and then: *!!!!*—and my head feels like a hot air balloon and balloons hold in air too, never meaning to let it out, and of course that makes kids' birthday parties full of bright round things full and about to burst and sometimes they do, so yeah, as a kid, those get togethers were not really a good thing for me, right, and that can really affect the social life in elementary school—like the one *that* teacher toils at, the one with the *Riverview* lanyard sliding left and right against her soft neck flesh as she feels the ankle biters close around her and press in from all sides, and I picture those kids going up to the mechanic saying *Whatcha doin' mister?* and him getting all distracted as they approach and him pressing some lever that's not meant to be pressed right there, right then, and that car slamming down on top of them all, flattening them like sandwiches.

And the idea of sandwiches makes me hungry, and me being hungry makes me thirsty, and so I decide to search out some prey of my own—like a sandwich and a drink—and I won't inhale them whole or do anything that might make me choke or drown and you know the fear of drowning, that's what most people think is aquaphobia, but aquaphobia is the fear of water, so that's not quite the same, and thalassophobia, that's the fear of large bodies of water, so that's not quite the same, so strangely enough, there's no name for fear of drowning, and maybe if Ophelia had a healthy fear of drowning or a healthy fear of water, she never would have drowned in that *Hamlet* play we studied back in grade twelve, but that's all to say that drowning might be a lot like fear of suffocation, like something pressing in on your rib cage and lungs, some pressure you don't want *there*, and that's like claustrophobia, and it's the reason I've been through CBT and REBT and relaxation and visualization and exposure therapy and medication and you name it for what I've got, but all those are just nice names for psychotherapy, which isn't such a nice word and makes it sound like you're a raving lunatic psycho serial killer on the loose, which probably isn't the case at all and certainly isn't the case with me.

And the rest of my walk, I notice things—lawns with chain link fences, closing them off, dogs with collars and bandanas around their throats, and them not being able to complain a bit about it, and some owners tugging on the leashes to make it hurt even more, and it's then that I feel shooting stars and gunfire and fireworks exploding under my ribs and inside my heart—*bdm!bdm!bdm!—!!!*—and I see it, my narrow escape, and it doesn't come too soon—my fave café—and my heart is pounding so hard I hear it, so no coffee for me, nosiree, so I order a refresher instead, the purple dragon fruit one that soothes me smoothly, and I sit with my back to the window, so I don't see the crowd outside, and I sit facing the corner, so I don't see the crowd inside.

And there's a newspaper on the table, the *Calgary Herald*, and when you think about it, the covers of the paper trap the other pages inside, don't they, the same way Calgary's province, Alberta, is trapped between British Columbia and Saskatchewan, trapped on two sides, well, and the territories above and the US below, so really, four sides like an elevator, so I try not to think about that and I snap the pages open to the national news, and the first headline I see kinda does a shimmy and a shake and things keep moving and shifting like a quake, and that's when I kinda know I'm in trouble:

Overfishing of hundreds of thousands of BC-bound
sockeye by Alaskan fishers (off Noyes Island)
Overfishing of hundreds of thousands of BC-
bound sockeye (by Alaskan fishers)
Overfishing of hundreds of thousands of
(BC-bound) sockeye
Overfishing of hundreds (of
thousands) of sockeye
Overfishing (of hundreds) of sockeye
Overfishing (of sockeye)
Overfish(ing)
Over(fish)
O(ver)
(O)
()
!
.

BOOK CLUB GUIDE

A Baker's Dozen of Duos

If you are meeting with a book club to discuss some of the stories in *The Killing Jar*, allow me to give you a few ideas of where to start. Often, it's easiest to compare. With that in mind, here are a Baker's dozen pairings (12 + 1) to get you going:

1. Jars are used in "Cookie Monster" and "The Killing Jar." In both of these stories, I use the jars to provide some structure—to create links between the beginning, the middle, and the end. Your thoughts?

2. Crosses are used symbolically in both "Cookie Monster" and "Flashmob Fisherwoman." What do you notice?

3. With that in mind, how are creatures—a chameleon and a frog—used in "Chameleon" and "Menos Coca, Más Cacao"?

4. Two of the stories—"Flashmob Fisherwoman" and "The High Price of Fish"—mention fish in the titles. For which of the stories is it a more important image? Why?

5. If you notice, the SAME farm tragedy is included in both “Plow Breaks Soil” and “Seven Shadows.” This is because it is based on a TRUE story from my life (when I was actually much younger than a university student, ahem). For which of the stories does that stuck calf incident have more of an impact?

6. Colombia and Singapore? I’m Canadian, so these exotic locales demanded research, one which I did in person, the other through reading. Which setting impacts choices made in the storytelling more, in your view?

7. Related to #6, look at the protagonists in “The Killing Jar” and “Menos Coca, Mas Cacao,” one Japanese, the other Colombian. If writers include people of different ethnicities as major characters in their work, they are often accused of cultural appropriation. If they DON’T include any type of major character of a different ethnicity in their work, they could be called racist. Thoughts? (Interesting side note: both of these stories were entered into writing contests where they were judged “blind”—my name was not attached to the story. In both cases, they won the contests. More food for thought?)

8. Incest and murder. These are some particularly nasty parts of life dealt with in “(Don’t)Connect the Dots” and “My Singapore Garden,” to name a

few. How do you find the treatment of those topics in these works?

9. Poetry in the prose. In "The Killing Jar" and "Seven Shadows," my characters make use of poetry as therapy in a way. What do you think about the blend of poetry and prose in the telling of each tale? Effects?

10. Twist endings, anyone? In one case, a male gold-digger, sort of a reverse stereotype. In another, a creative murder weapon used to exact revenge. What do you think of the denouements of "Build It Up Right" and "Menos Coca, Más Cacao"?

11. Distinctive voices. I've been told again and again that it's important to have your characters have their own unique voices. What can you say about the protagonists of "Narrow Escape" and "Cookie Monster"?

12. Strong female protagonists. I almost always write my stories using a female protagonist, even though I am male. This is on purpose—writing as a female tends to make the character more fictional and unique and less like my own voice (although that still creeps through in places). Which two stories have the strongest females?

+1 Plus one.

Another tossed in to make a Baker's dozen (just like the origin of the term). Let's get nostalgic. "Cookie

Monster" came from memories I have of one of my favourite *Sesame Street* characters. "Clue" was based on one of my favourite board games of the same name. Take a moment to talk about YOU. What are favourites from your childhood, items, places, characters and people you've held onto?

An offer to book clubs:

You've invested in my book. Let me offer you something in return. If you live in Vancouver or the Lower Mainland like I do, send me an invitation to the day you'll meet to discuss some of the stories. I'll do my best to crash your party.

Is Zoom preferable or necessary because of where you live? I can do that too. Who knows? I might even have a little bonus to leave with you because of your kindness... a story that's not in the collection.

Contact me at writeracebaker@gmail.com and we'll take it from there...

ABOUT THE AUTHOR

Ace Baker is a writer, poet, and writing coach from Vancouver, Canada. His short story, "Victory Girl," won the Storyteller Award, and another, "Menos Coca, Más Cacao" won the *Blank Spaces* short fiction contest, "The Things We Leave Behind," and was published in an anthology by the same name. His poetry has won the SIWC, PNWA, and Magpie awards, among others. Both his prose and poetry have been nominated for the Pushcart Prize and National Magazine Awards.

ACKNOWLEDGEMENTS

"Victory Girl" ("The Killing Jar") won the SIWC Storyteller award in 2012 and was later published by *Pulp Literature* in Issue 4, Autumn 2014.

"Plow Breaks Soil" placed third in a *Blank Spaces* contest in 2019.

"The High Price of Fish" was a finalist (6th) in the mainstream / literary category of the *Writer's Digest* 82nd Annual Contest in 2013.

"Build It Up Right" was shortlisted for the SIWC Short Fiction Award in 2013.

"Menos Coca, Más Cacao" won *Blank Spaces*' "The Things We Left Behind" contest in April, 2022, and was published in a book by the same title with the other seven finalists.

"Don't Connect the Dots" was published by Red Tuque in *Canadian Tales of the Mysterious*, in 2012.

"Seven Shadows" was a finalist in PNWA in 2015.

Manufactured by Amazon.ca
Bolton, ON

35254416R00088